Blake put his fingers and gently tipped her head back.

He wanted to kiss this woman.

Wait. *What?*

No. That would be wild. He couldn't kiss her. Shouldn't.

Her hair tumbled off her shoulders and down her back in golden curls. Before he knew it, his free hand was slowly twisting into those curls. She didn't pull away. Didn't look away. He lowered his head until his face was just above hers. Her lips parted and she stared at him with her enormous eyes.

"I swear I don't want to scare you, Amanda. But... may I kiss you?" His voice was a raw whisper. "Please."

His words came out as a plea. He'd never begged for anything before in his life. But here he was, begging this sweet woman for a kiss. Ready to drop to his knees if that's what it took. He started to straighten; started to come to his senses. Then he heard her whispered answer.

"Yes."

Adrenaline surged through his body, and his hand tightened in her hair. His eyes opened to meet those two oceans of blue. Dangerous blue. Deep enough to drown in.

She was frightened, but she was trusting him. And that realization scared *him* to death.

GALLANT LAKE STORIES: At home on the water!

Dear Reader,

Do you believe in time travel? I hope so, because this origin story takes us back, but only a couple of years. Blake and Amanda have appeared as a couple in all my Lowery Women series books and in the first Gallant Lake Stories book. Readers wanted to know their story, and I'm thrilled to share it with you.

It was Blake Randall's arrival in the Catskills town of Gallant Lake, after purchasing the Gallant Lake Resort and the neighboring historic home named Halcyon, that started the rebirth of the town. Although, thanks to a pesky local legend, things don't unfold the way Blake originally planned.

Blake hires interior designer Amanda Lowery to do *something* with the old castle he'd originally planned to demolish. The nervous blonde turns his plans—and his life—upside down. He's a man who doesn't believe in love. She's a woman afraid to trust. When Blake's young nephew shows up on the doorstep, they all start a journey toward becoming a family, just in time for Christmas.

The fictional castle, Halcyon, was inspired by several *real* castles in New York State. Some were built as gifts from men of the Gilded Age to their wives—talk about swoonworthy heroes! My thanks to the people who have preserved magnificent properties like Boldt Castle, Singer Castle, Belhurst Castle and others. Please visit them, or local historic homes, if you have the opportunity.

Happy holidays!

Jo McNally

It Started
at Christmas...

—

Jo McNally

HHARLEQUIN® SPECIAL EDITION

Recycling programs
for this product may
not exist in your area.

ISBN-13: 978-1-335-57427-5

It Started at Christmas…

Copyright © 2019 by Jo McNally

Printed in U.S.A.

www.Harlequin.com

Jo McNally lives in coastal North Carolina with one hundred pounds of dog and two hundred pounds of husband—her slice of the bed is very small. When she's not writing or reading romance novels (or clinging to the edge of the bed), she can often be found on the back porch sipping wine with friends while listening to great music. If the weather is absolutely perfect, Jo might join her husband on the golf course, where she tends to feel far more competitive than her actual skill level would suggest.

She likes writing stories about strong women and the men who love them. She's a true believer that love can conquer all if given just half a chance.

You can follow Jo pretty much anywhere on social media (and she'd love it if you did!), but you can start at her website, jomcnallyromance.com.

Books by Jo McNally

Harlequin Special Edition

Gallant Lake Stories

A Man You Can Trust

Harlequin Superromance

Nora's Guy Next Door
She's Far From Hollywood

HQN

Rendevous Falls

Slow Dancing at Sunrise
Stealing Kisses in the Snow

Visit the Author Profile page
at Harlequin.com for more titles.

This book is dedicated to my smart, talented, funny agent, Veronica Park,
for never giving up on this story of my heart.

Prelude

Three days after Christmas...

Big fat snowflakes swirled through the air at the cemetery, making everything look fuzzy three days after the worst Christmas ever. Zachary watched the people walk back to their cars. Big piles of flowers surrounded his mother's grave.

"Do you think Mom sent the snow?"

"What?" Uncle Blake looked down at Zachary and frowned.

"Maybe...maybe Mom sent the snow. Like a message or something. She taught me how to catch snowflakes on my tongue, like this..." Zachary stuck his tongue out. A white flake landed, melting in a quick, cold burst. Uncle Blake's face screwed up like he'd just stepped on a Lego, but Zach rushed on. "Remember how much she loved Christmas, Uncle Blake? Maybe she's still here, but you can't see her... like the ghost of Christmas future in that story—"

"No." His uncle's voice sounded rough and scratchy. "She's not here, Zach. Your mom isn't a ghost. She's just... gone."

He meant Mom was dead. Zach wasn't stupid. He knew what dead meant. What he didn't get was, why wouldn't people just say it?

Uncle Blake looked up at the snow for a minute. "She loved Christmas so much because it's for little kids, and she never stopped... She never really grew up." He knelt in front of Zach, one knee in the snow. "I know this was a lousy holiday, and I'm sorry. I miss her, too. But you're going to have to be a man now. You need to leave make-believe for the little kids, okay?"

Zach straightened his shoulders. He missed his mom. She was funny, and she gave the best hugs ever. Hugs that made him feel safe, even in the middle of another move or if she was changing boyfriends again. And now he'd never have another hug from her. He blinked his eyes. Would anyone ever hug him like that? Probably not. Hugs were like Christmas—for little kids only. He looked into his uncle's eyes and nodded.

He wasn't really sure how to be a man, but if that's what his uncle wanted, he'd try.

Chapter One

"This has got to be the stupidest thing I've ever done."

"What? The shopping or the job?"

Amanda Lowery juggled the bags in her hand, laughing at her cousin's question.

"Both, I guess. There's no way I'll get the job after Mr. Randall meets me tomorrow, which means I won't be able to pay for any of this stuff."

The two women stood on the sidewalk in Gallant Lake, New York. Like so many upstate villages, a lot of the brick or clapboard storefronts were empty. There were still a few businesses left, and they'd managed to shop in every one of them. There was just a hint of color starting to show in the mountains surrounding the lake, which glittered in the afternoon sun. Labor Day was just over a week away. Soon those trees would be ablaze in the reds and golds of autumn. Amanda and Mel were standing in front of a colorful coffee shop directly across the road from a tiny park overlooking the lake.

"Hey, you got this final interview fair and square…" Mel grimaced. "Well, not exactly *fair*, but you know what I mean. You're the one who came up with the plans the guy liked."

"Yes, but he thinks those plans came from *David*, not me. He's expecting a *man* to show up tomorrow morning. Like I said—stupid." She looked up at the bright orange coffee shop door. "Come on, let's get a cappuccino before we head back to the resort."

After ordering, they settled in at a table by the window.

The café was small, but there weren't many people inside, so Amanda didn't have to worry about her personal space. Their table was bright blue. The chairs were each a different color. Nothing in the place matched, creating a chaotic, but energetic, atmosphere. As a designer, Amanda would describe the look as bohemian eclectic. Local artwork on the brick walls displayed widely varying degrees of talent. The place smelled of roasted coffee beans, cinnamon and sawdust. The latter was courtesy of the woodworking shop next door.

"Amanda, once this Randall guy meets you and hears that you specialize in historic homes and how many projects you've already managed, he'll forget all about that little 'mix-up' and hire you on the spot." Mel smiled and pushed her dark hair behind an ear. Two older men sitting near the counter were openly staring at her, but Mel was used to it. She had cheekbones most women would kill for. And legs that went on forever. And violet eyes that evoked memories of Elizabeth Taylor. Amanda sighed, glancing down at her short legs and...um...curvy figure. Genetics were tricky. That's why Mel was a former supermodel, while women like Amanda ended up working behind the scenes with furniture and fabric.

"It wasn't a mix-up, Mel. It was *intentional*. I'm a *deceiver*." She was so desperate for this job that she'd resorted to unethical business practices. That was *so* not who she was. But a woman had to eat, right?

Mel waved off her concerns—easy to do when you were rich and famous. "I wonder what these signs are about? I've been seeing them all over town."

Mel pointed at a cardboard sign in the window with the word *casino* across the front in black, and a giant red circle and diagonal line over it. Amanda hadn't noticed, too occupied with worrying about tomorrow.

The café's owner brought their cappuccinos to the table.

She was an older woman, with long salt-and-pepper hair and a heavy skirt that doubled as a floor sweeper. There was no doubt where the hippie vibe of the coffee shop came from.

"Here you go, honeys. My name's Cathy. Anything else I can getcha?"

Mel pointed to the sign. "What's the story with that?"

Cathy's smile faded. "Bad news for Gallant Lake." She shook her head, lips pressed together. "Some big-shot developer bought the old resort a couple years ago, and instead of fixing it up like we'd hoped, he wants to tear it down and build a damned casino. A *casino*! I mean, what is this, New Jersey? Are we going to be living in one of those De Niro movies now?" Cathy's face twisted in disgust. "We're fighting him, though. No way do we want some giant sign of a neon bimbo here in our town, kicking her leg at the sky."

Mel smirked, and Amanda knew what she was thinking. Clearly, someone hadn't been to Vegas lately. Not all casinos were gaudy and gauche. On a more selfish note, Amanda wondered if they'd hired a decorator yet.

"The Gallant Lake Resort?" Mel said. "That's where we're staying. It seems nice." The sprawling four-story stone-and-timber hotel hugged the shoreline of the lake. The decor might be kitschy and straight out of the sixties, but the place was clean and the views were wonderful.

"Yeah, the family that used to own it always took good care of the place. But they could never afford to remodel. Still, there's no need to tear it down."

Amanda looked out the window at Main Street, dotted with puddles from last night's rain. She saw several boarded-up storefronts. "Wouldn't a casino bring in more jobs and tourists?"

Cathy shrugged. "But at what cost? That resort's history is a part of us. Old Blue Eyes himself used to sing there!

The whole Rat Pack did. Streisand sang for the governor's birthday party once. People would come up here from the city and boy, would they spend money!" Cathy brushed some dust off the windowsill with the corner of her apron. "The old resorts are being torn down all over the Catskills, and we don't want to lose ours." She perched on the edge of a nearby table. Mel smiled, as if enjoying the small-town lack of pretense. "We think if it was spruced up and advertised more, it would bring vacationers back to Gallant Lake again. Maybe the old ski resort would reopen. And the golf course. Business would pick up for everyone."

"But wouldn't a nice new casino do the same thing?" Amanda couldn't stand to be in a casino herself, with people pressing in from everywhere. Just thinking about it made her palms sweat. But if it would bring business to the obviously struggling town...

"Ha! The operative word is *nice*. Mr. Hotshot wants to build some ugly ten-story high-rise on our beautiful lake. Main Street will be nothing more than a thoroughfare from the highway to his casino. That won't help *my* business. He's buying up houses just to turn them into parking lots. Parking lots!" Cathy laughed and winked. "Of course, we stopped him from turning *one* of them into a parking lot. We had his big old house declared a landmark and now he's stuck with it! That boy picked the wrong little town to mess with."

Cathy was still cackling when she walked away. Mel gave a low whistle. "Whoever that guy is, I hope he doesn't buy his coffee here. I'm pretty sure Cathy would spit in it."

Amanda giggled, then reached over to squeeze her cousin's hand.

"Thanks for coming with me this weekend, Mel. Whatever happens with the job interview tomorrow, it'll be easier to handle the fallout with you here." She was pretty sure she knew exactly what was going to happen. She was going to be sent packing. Her stomach clenched. It would be exactly what she deserved.

"You'll do great, kid," Mel said. "No matter who he's *expecting*, he liked the plans you sent, and he's going to like you, too."

Her cousin had no idea how close Amanda was to giving up and going home to her mother's house in Nowheresville, Kansas, with her tail tucked between her legs—a failure.

"I hope so. If I can get a showcase job like this, it might be enough to start my own solo business." It would also save her from slinking back home in disgrace after once again trusting the wrong guy. "We should get back to the resort."

"Yeah, I want to look at that purse you found at the antiques shop. I still say that little key was for a really fancy chastity belt."

Amanda smiled. Despite her budget woes, she'd found something she couldn't resist buying. She'd fallen in love with the vintage beaded evening bag from the 1920s. To her delight, she'd discovered a tiny ornate key tucked inside. She and Mel had made up some hysterical possibilities for what that key might unlock.

They grabbed their bags and headed to the rental car parked across the street. Mel was giving another lecture on how Amanda was worrying too much about things. Amanda did her best to tune it out because discussing her worry didn't make her worry any less.

Mel grabbed Amanda's arm with a cry as she stepped off the sidewalk. An enormous black SUV sped by, too close to the curb. It hit a puddle, and before Amanda could react, she was drenched. The jerk barely slowed down before speeding off around the corner.

"Son of a bitch!" Amanda jumped back and turned to Mel, who, of course, was perfectly dry. She was also doubled over with laughter.

Amanda looked down. Her pink sweater clung to her,

and water dripped off her fingertips. She wanted to be mad. She *was* mad. But when she looked up and found Mel still giggling, wiping tears from her eyes, Amanda couldn't help but join her. If there was an edge of hysteria to her laughter, who could blame her?

They were still laughing when they got back to the resort. Mel insisted that they walk right through the lobby with all their packages, despite Amanda's soggy footprints.

"Cathy said they're tearing the place down anyway, so what difference does it make?"

"Nathan, are you kidding me?" Blake Randall pressed harder on the gas and sent his SUV roaring up the country road approaching Gallant Lake. "You took our nephew to school a week early so you could take your girls on vacation *without* him? Who the hell *does* that to a ten-year-old kid?"

Blake floored it past farms, double-wides and large Victorian homes. His hands gripped the wheel so tight he was surprised it didn't snap.

"I've had Zachary all summer, Blake," his brother whined over the speakerphone. "Michaela wanted some time with *our* family."

"He *is* your damned family!" He and Nathan were the only family Zach had left. Their father wouldn't even acknowledge the boy's existence, so that left him and Nathan to give Zach a sense of family. Even if it was a thoroughly dysfunctional one.

"You know what I mean." He could hear Nathan taking a deep breath. His older brother always did that when he was trying to find the balls to challenge Blake. "Look, *you're* his guardian. We took him for the summer, but it wasn't a permanent thing."

"But you already have a family." Nathan was a father. A questionable one, perhaps, but still. At least he wasn't as clueless about kids as Blake was. "Why can't you add one more?"

"Not happening, Blake. Tiffany named you in her will. Not me."

"Only because she and Michaela hated each other." Tiffany used to refer to Nathan's wife as Butt Stick. Blake's lips twitched at the memory of him and his sister laughing over that name.

"And yet you think Michaela should raise Tiffany's kid. What *sense* does that make?"

Nathan had a point. Blake had qualms about Michaela raising her *own* children. As if Blake was some kind of expert.

"He shouldn't be at Beakman Academy by himself, a week ahead of the other kids."

"The upperclassmen are there this week," Nathan sighed. "The headmaster said he'd be fine."

Blake slowed to pass a farm tractor driving up the road. Was that thing even legal? He stepped on the gas after he passed it, going too fast for being this close to the village. Sheriff Adams must have been busy somewhere else because Blake didn't see any flashing lights. Benefits of a one-cop town.

"So Zach's at school with a bunch of kids *four grades* ahead of him? That's perfect, genius. What could *possibly* go wrong?"

"Jesus, Blake, I'm not an idiot. He's not in the dorm—he's staying with the headmaster and his family for the week. Feel free to drive over and get him if you don't like it."

Blake chewed his lip. Zach was ten years old. He'd lost his mother less than a year ago. Blake had a feeling *everything* was a big deal to the poor kid. But still…being at school gave him more structure than he'd have with Blake, or even Nathan and Butt Stick.

"Can you guys at least take him for the holiday break?" Tiffany had died at Christmas. Zach deserved a much happier holiday this year.

"No way. We're taking the girls on a cruise for Christmas, and Michaela already said—"

"Yeah, yeah. I can imagine what Michaela said." Blake let off the gas pedal and hung up on his brother. He reached for his coffee and bit out a curse when some spilled on his pants. What a perfect freakin' day. He saw a flash of pink when he looked up and swore again. A petite blonde stepped off the sidewalk, directly into his path.

Blake swerved. The engine on the big vehicle roared. He'd drifted pretty damned close to the curb, scaring the daylights out of himself and no doubt her. After he passed, he glanced in the rearview mirror and winced. He'd hit a puddle and sent a tidal wave of water over her. She was stomping her feet and gesturing to the taller woman behind her, pushing long, wet hair out of her face.

A nice person would have stopped and apologized. But Blake had learned the hard way that being nice in Gallant Lake got him nowhere. He was not popular, and he'd only attract an angry mob if anyone saw him stopped in the middle of town. He felt bad about ruining the woman's afternoon, though. Driving away without stopping made him feel uncomfortably similar to the ogre some of the locals painted him as. He didn't like it.

Speaking of angry mobs, there were five or six picketers just setting up at the entrance to his resort. The small Gallant Lake Preservation Society liked to show up with their handwritten signs, especially if they knew Blake was in town. They loved telling him, loudly and often, that they "weren't giving up the fight" when it came to his plans for the casino. They didn't seem to realize the town had given up on itself years before. That had nothing to do with him. Their signs proclaimed the same old mantra.

Save Gallant Lake!

No Casino!

Leave Our Lake Alone!

They were usually well behaved and didn't interfere with resort traffic. But guests would be asking questions. He saw a scruffy pair of guys at the edge of the group. They didn't fit in with the generally older protesters, but it wasn't the first time he'd seen them hanging around. The two always looked ready to take up torches and pitchforks rather than neatly lettered signs. Their anger simmered a little closer to the surface, like it was personal, but Blake had no idea who they were.

The group recognized his vehicle and pressed closer to the entrance, forcing him to slow down to avoid hitting them. He could call the sheriff, but that wouldn't do any good. The protestors always stayed back off his property lines when the guy they affectionately called "Sheriff Dan" was around. Blake had a sneaking suspicion the sheriff supported the locals more than him when it came down to it.

Once past the entrance, he parked in the employee lot and came in the side door. The old place had character, along with a stellar view. The previous owners had maintained the resort well, even if the interior needed updating *everywhere*. Those updates would be pointless now since it was slated for demolition as soon as the state senate gave its blessing to the casino plans. He was only a few votes away.

When he'd made the purchase originally, sight unseen, he'd assumed the resort was one of those tired old Catskills resorts whose glory days ended with the *Dirty Dancing* era. It was a pleasant surprise to see the place actually making a little money with a modest marketing campaign, which took some of the sting out of waiting for those last few votes.

It was smaller than his other hotels, but he ran it with the same attention to detail. He was known for his No Surprises approach to business, and the employees here had been quick to catch on—they took care of little problems *before* they became big ones.

He saw the muddy footprints as soon as he entered the lobby on his way to the front desk. *What the hell?* The sun was shining outside, but this looked like someone had walked through here after swimming in a ditch somewhere. He caught a glimpse of pink ahead, stepping inside the elevator. Well, he'd be damned. The blonde he'd almost mowed down in town was a guest at the resort.

It seemed she'd rewarded his behavior with a trail of mud across the lobby carpet, almost as if she knew it was his place. Blake couldn't help the smile that tugged at his mouth. It served him right for not stopping to apologize.

Chapter Two

Amanda paused by the lobby windows to settle her nerves. The resort's lawn swept down to the lakeshore. A morning mist rose from the water still in the shadows of the mountain. Resting the palm of her hand against her stomach, she focused her energy on pulling air in and letting it out. *In with the good air, out with the bad.* She'd hardly slept all night, and her nerves were jangling so much she could practically hear them rattling in her head.

She held a cup of coffee in her other hand—one last boost of caffeinated courage. Counterintuitive to her attempt to calm down? Maybe. But she needed to be sharp. It was almost time for her to meet Blake Randall and inform him that he'd been corresponding with someone other than her ex-boss. That he'd sent blueprints for his historic mansion to *her*, not David Franklin. His request for proposals asked for suggestions on how to put the building to use, preferably as a commercial space, with no indication where it was actually located or what the exterior looked like. It was all very mysterious. When she "accidentally" intercepted the RFP and *intentionally* responded, she'd provided plans for *residential* use instead. She loved period architecture and felt the home should be used for its original purpose.

Randall had liked her plans enough to request a meeting to discuss them. Her shoulders straightened. They were *her* ideas, and they were good ones. What did it matter who they came from? She tried to dismiss the panic fluttering in her chest. She could do this. She *had* to do this. This job was the key to her being able to start her own design firm. One where she didn't have to rely on lying, cheating bosses who preyed on their employees.

Her summer had been almost laughable in its horridness. The panic attacks were happening more frequently. Nightmares left her afraid to go to sleep. She jumped at every little thing. No wonder her nerves were on a razor's edge. She felt like a canvas left out in the sun too long—stretched and dry and brittle.

She turned away from the windows and nearly collided with a guy in a Gallant Lake T-shirt and shorts. The twenty-something came out of nowhere, arguing loudly on the phone with someone about a canceled flight and a job he needed to get back to. Even though he'd nearly knocked her on her ass, the guy barely mumbled an apology before he continued on his way.

The brief, but forceful, male contact set off all kinds of alarms for Amanda. Black spots swirled at the edge of her vision.

A panic attack, her all-too-familiar companion these days, was prowling just under her skin, like a shark smelling blood. *Crap.* This was the last thing she needed this morning, but ignoring it would only give it more power. She set down her coffee and closed her eyes, trying to relax her muscles one group at a time, from her toes to her head, the way her therapist, Dr. Jackson, taught her.

In with the good air, out with the bad.

Shake off the negative while embracing the positive. So very much easier said than done. But she worked at it, picturing clean, fresh, strong air filling her lungs. She wiggled her fingers and rolled her shoulders. The monster quieted. It was time for her to get going.

Randall's cryptic instructions said to ask for directions to "Halcyon" at the front desk. She was surprised to get walking directions to a place right next door to the resort.

She headed outside and up the clearly marked path into the woods and through a gate in an old iron fence. A few minutes later, she stepped into a clearing and froze. Set high on a hill to her right was a *castle*. An honest-to-goodness castle, right there in the Catskills.

Her mouth fell open. She blinked. Then blinked again, as if she expected the sight to vanish. Another strange emotion swirled through her amazement, creating a wave of goose bumps across her skin. She couldn't believe what she was looking at. And yet…it felt as if she'd been here before. That was crazy. Randall had kept the location a deep dark secret in his proposal request. All she'd seen was the first floor blueprint.

The sense of déjà vu was overwhelming. The big house called to her so strongly that she could feel it in her bones, drawing her in like a siren call.

Pink granite walls rose from the ground as if the structure had just grown there. It seemed a natural part of the landscape, in spite of its soft color. It was at least three stories tall, with a sharply angled slate roof dotted with dormers. Two round towers anchored the lakeside corners, complete with pointed roofs like upside-down ice cream cones. There appeared to be another larger tower in the front of the house. A stone veranda stretched across the back, with five sets of French doors opening onto it.

The floor plans hadn't done this place justice. Halcyon was breathtaking. Amanda walked around to the front, noting signs of decades of neglect—overgrown shrubbery, dusty windows with no drapes and a general air of abandonment. The driveway circled around a long-forgotten and empty fountain. She walked up the stone stairs to the covered porch. The scale of everything made her feel like Alice in Wonderland, especially as she approached a massive wooden door. There wasn't a doorbell. She smiled to herself. The only appropriate doorbell for this place would be one you rang by pulling on a long velvet cord.

Amanda knocked, but there was no answer. She looked to the driveway. There weren't any cars there. She knocked again, using the side of her fist this time. Still nothing. She walked back around to the lake side of the house, looking for any signs of life. It had to be the right place, but why wasn't anyone here?

Up on the veranda, she paused to take in the view. The huge yard was surrounded by trees all the way to the water, and the only sound was that of the wind and the birds. It gave the feeling of being far removed from the world. When she turned to face the house, she noticed one of the doors stood ajar. Her skin prickled.

Maybe Mr. Randall was running late, and left the door open for her? Or maybe this was an elaborate ruse for someone to get a defenseless woman into an abandoned house, the monster whispered. Her pulse ratcheted up another notch.

No. She'd been corresponding as David Franklin, so no one was expecting a female. As long as she was here, and the door was open, why not explore? If Randall didn't show up, she'd head back to the resort and consider the missed appointment as karmic retribution for all of her lies.

Her footsteps left prints in the dust on the floor. She crouched down to wipe the dust away. The floors were honey-colored marble. The high coffered ceilings were made from mahogany. The walls bore some truly hideous Victorian wallpaper with flowers and gazebos and birds and...just way too much stuff. The massive fireplace was topped with a wooden mantel that stretched to the ceiling with an ornate carved scene of Saint George slaying a dragon. There were only a few pieces of furniture in the large room, and they were covered with drop cloths.

She wanted to see more of the house, and she *had* been

invited—sort of—but she still felt like she was trespassing. She caught a glimpse of massive iron chandeliers in the large room in the center of the house. Maybe just one quick look.

This house was sensory overload for a designer like her. Light flooded through tall leaded windows in the center hall. Twin iron chandeliers hung above her, with their curving black metal forms arching over the hall like protective birds of prey. The fireplace here was more subdued than in the other room, covered in the same golden marble as the floor and carved with a rose motif. She traced her fingers along the mantel, wondering what stories it could tell.

That's why she loved old homes so much—each one held a unique story. New homes had "potential," but she preferred a house with *history*. Someone had spared no expense a hundred years ago to create this beautiful space. And now it stood empty and smelled of dust and disuse. She absently patted her hand on the roses carved in marble, feeling sympathy for the sad old house.

She heard something that sounded as if it came from inside the house. Footsteps?

"Hello? Mr. Randall?"

There was only silence in reply. It must have been the wind she heard. Or perhaps it was just her overactive imagination kicking into high gear. She shrugged it off and continued exploring. Next to the front door, a stairway wound its way up the inside of the large tower. On the far side of the room, a semicircular glass atrium stretched across the end of the house. The glass was cloudy with age and neglect, and the mosaic floor covered with long-undisturbed dirt, but the atrium had been spectacular at one time.

The sketches she'd sent with her proposal were in black and white, created in a software program specifically for that purpose. They were filled with structural and furniture dimensions, accompanied with detailed lists of required supplies. They were accurate. But she knew now they weren't enough. Not for this house. Plans for this house needed color and emotion.

Amanda rested her hand on the paneled wall near the atrium, then closed her eyes and tried to get a feel for what the house might have looked like originally. It was a trick she'd used before to get a sense of the older apartments in the city she'd been hired to decorate. If only walls actually *could* talk. She pictured the atrium sparkling with candlelight, the metalwork along the roof painted bright white and the colorful floors restored. Exotic rugs scattered across the floor of the salon, creating cozy sitting areas by the fireplace and in front of the library. Lush but comfortable furniture filled this room and the living room. Everything she pictured reflected a sense of family and love.

None of that had been reflected in her proposal to Blake Randall. She pulled her ever-present sketchbook out of her bag, along with a fistful of colored pencils. She didn't have a lot of time, but she had to try to capture the personality of this home.

She lost herself in the drawing process, letting her creative muse take over. Flipping the pages hurriedly, she sketched the salon, then the dining room, which she'd envisioned as a home office. Eventually she went back to the living room, imagining it with touches of modern technology mixed with classic colors and...oh, wouldn't sailcloth curtains be perfect in here!

She heard another noise, and stopped her frantic sketching. She was sure it came from *inside* the house. Was it from upstairs, or the room next door? She tucked her sketchbook back into her bag and headed for the open door to the veranda, ready to flee if needed. Her pulse pounded in her ears. Was that a footstep behind her?

"Hey!" The loud male voice stopped her in her tracks. Panic slammed her heart against her ribs, and her vision blurred. Before she could force her feet to move, a large hand gripped her upper arm and a deep voice growled at her.

"What the hell are you doing in my house?"

Sometimes her panic manifested itself as rage, and she was thankful for that rage right now. It was the only thing keeping her on her feet. Instead of fainting dead away, she yanked her arm free and turned to face the man who'd just sent her panic levels into the stratosphere. Her knees threatened to buckle. Breathing felt like a battle between her lungs and the air she needed.

"Don't *touch* me!" she said with a hiss.

He released her immediately, but he was now blocking her exit. He was older than her—maybe midthirties— and tall. She was wearing heels, and still her head barely reached his shoulders. His features were sharp and his jaw strong. His eyes were the color of espresso, and thick black hair curled down the nape of his neck. He was dressed casually, as if he'd been working outside and just walked in.

She swallowed hard and tried to control her pounding pulse. She'd read once that the tiniest animal, when cornered, could become ferocious beyond its physical size. She drew herself to her full height, ignoring the barest hint of a smile that flickered across the man's face when she pointed her finger and started lecturing.

"You'd better get out of here while you still have the chance, because Blake Randall will be here any minute now to meet me!"

His right brow arched sharply, but instead of leaving, he leaned back against the door frame and folded his arms on his chest, a wide smile on his face.

"Is that right? Blake Randall? Well, that's interesting. Because *my* appointment is with a gentleman, not a nosy, trespassing woman."

Amanda's mouth fell open. *This* was Blake Randall. And

she was an idiot. She'd just blown any possibility of getting the job that was her last hope. The thought of crawling back to Kansas in defeat made her skin tight and clammy. She stepped back and bumped against the door, stumbling when it swung further open behind her. She hated this feeling of her feet being encased in cement every time she panicked, leaving her clumsy and slow.

"Jesus, relax." His voice lost some of its growl. "I'm just sick of people trying to sneak into this place like it's some shrine instead of being private property. What do you want?"

Amanda's lungs were rapidly constricting. *In with the good air, out with the bad.* She was having a hard time envisioning anything good in this situation. He ran long fingers through his hair, clearly running out of patience. She blew out another breath and her vision cleared. Her voice only trembled a little.

"You're Blake Randall?" She did her best not to grimace when he nodded once in reply. "The door was open, Mr. Randall. I assumed you were inside. I'm your ten o'clock appointment." She knew she should hold her hand out, but her aversion to touch made her avoid handshakes at all costs. Maybe he wouldn't notice. "I'm Amanda Lowery."

He barked out a laugh. "Do you think I don't know who my appointment is with? It's with—"

"David Franklin of Franklin Interiors. Yes, I know. I used to work with David. I was an associate at the firm. I'm the one who responded to your email." Someone at the office had taken a little too long closing her email account after she'd left. Randall's email had seemed like a gift—an answer to her prayers—when it showed up in her inbox a month ago.

"You responded *as* David Franklin."

"I responded as a representative of the firm." What she'd done was beyond unprofessional. Probably illegal. But she'd been desperate. She hadn't actually signed David's name to the emails, but she hadn't signed hers, either. She'd deceived this man. But what choice did she have after David smeared her reputation and left her unemployable?

"So you're here representing Franklin Interiors and their proposal?"

"Well…um…no. It was *my* proposal."

"So you work for another firm now, and you're trying to poach me from Franklin?"

"Not exactly. I'm…um…self-employed."

Panic started whispering more loudly in her head. This was a mistake. What if he called David? What if he called the police?

Instead, he just laughed. "Wow—you lost your job at Franklin Interiors." His gaze sharpened. "Fired or quit?"

"A little of both, I guess." When she'd confronted David for taking credit for her work, he'd slandered her with their clients. He and she had basically raced to get the words out after a client told her what he'd said. She was pretty sure her "I quit" beat his "you're fired" by a few seconds.

"And now you're bluffing your way into an interview for the renovation of a million-dollar mansion? You look like you're barely out of college." He stared at her for a long moment, and she just stared back, unsure if she should flee in embarrassment or stand and fight for the seemingly hopeless chance of getting this job. She pictured herself back in rural Kansas and straightened. She *had* to fight.

"I'm twenty-eight. I worked at Franklin for four years. I created the proposal that got your attention and led to this appointment. This house is magnificent, and I really ne—*want* this job."

He snorted. "Magnificent? This pile of rocks is a pain right in my ass."

Her panic was briefly forgotten. He had to be joking. This house was… She looked around and wondered once

again at the connection she felt to the dusty, neglected structure. This house…was where she needed to be. She *had*
to get this job. He hadn't thrown her out yet *or* called the
cops, so that was something. He looked around the room
as if trying to see what she saw.

"Everyone in town forced me to keep this place standing, but…"

Something clicked in her brain.

"Wait—is this the historic landmark they were talking
about saving?"

"*Who* was talking?"

"The lady who owns the coffee shop was telling my
cousin and me about it. She said some idiot wants to destroy the resort and a bunch of houses so he can build some
awful casino. Everyone in town hates the idea, and hates
the guy trying to…" Her voice faded off as she watched
a variety of emotions cross his face, from amusement to
anger to…regret? Her cheeks flamed. "And that guy would
be *you*, right? You own the resort, too?"

He gave her a mock bow. "Blake Randall, the villain
of Gallant Lake, at your service. But don't believe Cathy
when she says *everyone* hates the idea. The casino will
provide a lot of jobs for people around here if I can ever
get approval from Albany." He frowned. "Cathy and her
friends in the Gallant Lake Preservation Society managed
to have Halcyon declared a landmark, so I have to put it to
use, which is why I asked you…well, not *you*, apparently…
to give me a proposal. Another firm suggested convert-
ing this into an office building, and leasing out whatever
space we don't use."

"Using this house for offices would be criminal." She
might have been having the worst summer ever, but she
knew her stuff when it came to vintage homes like this. It
was her specialty, and her knowledge gave her a spark of

courage. "This was a family home once, full of love and laughter. It could be that kind of home again."

He looked at her as if she'd suddenly started speaking a foreign language. There was a spark of interest in his expression, but then he drew back and shook his head.

"Look, it took some guts to worm your way into an appointment under false pretenses, and I admire your ambition. But— "

"You liked my proposal just fine when you thought it came from Franklin Interiors. Have you suddenly stopped liking it?"

He shook his head. "Your proposal was the best one I received for residential use, but I'm not convinced a twelve-bedroom castle can ever really be a home." He looked around the dusty living room. "Even if I was, don't you think this project is a little over your head?"

"Why? Because I'm a woman?"

"No. Because you're young, you're alone and you can't possibly have the experience or the resources for a job like this."

His arms went wide, gesturing around the room, and she stepped back, rattled by the sudden movement. He wasn't going to hire her. There was no sense in begging. This had been her last hope, and she wasn't going to get the job. Tears gathered in the corners of her eyes. She'd have to go home to Kansas, where all her nightmares began.

She should get out of here now, while she still had some shred of dignity. She raised her chin, determined not to show him what a blow he was dealing her.

"It's clear your mind is made up. Excuse me." She moved toward the door, praying he'd just let her pass without coming any closer.

His brow arched high.

"That's it? You're not going to fight for the job after going through that elaborate ruse to get yourself here?"

This was nothing more than a game to him. He thought she was some nice young girl pretending to be a *real* designer. Wasn't that what David had called her? As much as she wanted to prove them both wrong, she had to leave. Now. There was a panic attack barreling down on her like a freight train, and she didn't want any witnesses. Especially one who already thought she was a poser.

She started to walk past him and out the door, but her feet refused to cooperate with her bravado, and she stumbled. *Damn it!* Out of the corner of her eye she saw him reaching for her. No!

Her arms flew out. He grabbed at her. *Shit!* She tried to push him away and break her fall at the same time, but she ended up on the stone floor, looking up at him as he gripped her shoulders.

"Careful! Are you o—" Their eyes met. "Miss Lowery? Amanda? Can you hear me?"

His hands were on her. His hands were *on* her! She couldn't speak. Couldn't move. Couldn't breathe. Her body trembled, making her head rattle against the marble floor. Her vision faded. The pain in her chest was so overwhelming she wondered if she was dying. She must have said as much, because a deep voice answered from much too close.

"You're not dying. You just need to breathe. Hold my hand and squeeze. Try to breathe."

"Can't…hurts… Panic attack…" Strong arms gathered her up.

No! But she didn't have the strength to struggle. Every ounce of energy was spent trying to pull oxygen into her lungs.

"Tell me how to help you." She could hear fear in his voice, and it raised her panic level even higher. She heard a keening wail of pain and realized it was her. Her lungs were on fire, and she could barely form words.

"Don't…touch me…"

A gruff burst of air blew across her cheek. "That's not an option."

She was moving, flying. Being carried. He was shifting her around and fishing for something in his pocket. Her breathing came in short, shallow gasps. She wasn't getting enough oxygen to hold on to consciousness.

From far away, she heard a disembodied voice and snippets of conversation.

"Julie?…yes, Amanda Lowery…staying at the resort… panic attack…at the house…" Amanda rested her head on a solid shoulder. It was almost a relief to give up her fight against the inevitable darkness. The last thing she heard were soft words against her cheek.

"You're okay. I've got you."

There was a fairy-tale princess sleeping in his bed, right down to the flowing locks of golden hair. She had the face of an angel. An angel princess. Blake scrubbed his hand down his face, leaning back in the tall chair.

"You keep doing that and you won't have any skin left on your face."

He glanced over his shoulder at Amanda Lowery's cousin standing behind him. He gave a soft, humorless laugh.

"It's been one hell of a morning, Mel."

The tall brunette leaned her hip against the back of his chair. "For all of us. The doctor said she's okay, though. He gave her a pill. She's just sleeping."

Sure, she was sleeping *now.* But an hour ago, she'd taken ten years off his life. The panic had consumed her like wildfire, and there hadn't been a damned thing he could do to stop it.

He'd carried her up to his room in Halcyon while calling Julie, the assistant manager of the resort. Within minutes, a pissed-off brunette charged into his upstairs suite, ready to rescue Amanda and accusing him of all kinds of things. Fortunately, Julie had been just a few minutes behind Mel, along with a doctor staying at the resort. Julie convinced Mel that Blake wasn't an ax murderer, and was actually the guy Amanda had an appointment with. Once Mel calmed down, she confirmed what Amanda had tried to tell him—that it had been a panic attack.

"Why were you so insistent on keeping her here?" Mel asked. "After you knew she'd tricked you into interviewing her?"

Mel sat carefully on the edge of the bed, looking first at Amanda and then at him. It had been no surprise when she'd reluctantly confirmed to Julie that she was the famous fashion model known as Mellie Low. Every move this dark-haired woman made was intentionally graceful, as if there was always a camera on her. If he was in the market for a relationship, she was far more his usual type than Amanda—tall, elegant and coolly confident. But he wasn't in the market. That wall he'd constructed around his heart after losing Tiffany was high and solid. Completely impenetrable. He relaxed back into the chair and met her questioning eyes calmly.

"I'm not a *monster*, Mel. She just about had a heart attack in my house, and nearly gave me one in the process." He dropped his voice. "I keep a few furnished rooms here for when I'm in town, so it made sense to bring her up here." He looked up and noted her skepticism. "At least it made sense at the time."

Mel studied him hard for a minute, and he felt sorry for anyone who got on the wrong side of this woman. Her eyes were sharp as razors. If she ever decided to be a cop, that violet glare would have suspects confessing their guts all over the place. She was trying to protect her cousin, and he respected that. It wasn't the kind of family *he'd* grown up in, but it was the way families were supposed to be.

"She's safe here, I promise."

Mel's shoulders relaxed a bit at his comment, raising a red flag in his mind.

"That hasn't always been the case, has it? She hasn't always been safe?"

"No." She hesitated a moment and glanced at Amanda before answering in a hushed voice. "She's had a tough summer. Lost her job. About to lose her share of a shared apartment. And she was…" Mel straightened as if she realized she was speaking out of turn.

"Someone hurt her," he said softly.

She pressed her lips together and shook her head, but Blake could see the truth in her eyes. Someone had put their hands on the pretty princess sleeping in his bed. That's why she told him not to touch her. Was it a boyfriend? A stranger? His fingers curled into fists against his legs.

"And the panic attacks?" Blake was trying hard not to care, but he couldn't stop asking questions.

"You've seen firsthand how bad they can be."

He nodded. When she'd first landed on the living room floor, he'd thought she was having a seizure. Then their eyes had met and he'd known she was trapped in some nightmare he had no part of. The glassy terror in her eyes would haunt him for a long time to come.

She'd been skittish before that, but he'd figured she was just feeling guilty about the little game she was playing. When she'd stumbled and he'd reached for her, there was nothing funny about the way she couldn't breathe, couldn't speak. She'd scared the hell out of him, that's for damned sure. He was *still* afraid. He couldn't shake it for some reason.

"How often does that happen?"

Mel shrugged. "It's a fairly new development, so I'm not sure."

"Is she getting help for it?"

She started to nod, then caught herself. "That's none of your business."

Amanda *was* getting help. That was good. But Mel was right. It wasn't his concern.

Amanda moved, and he and Mel froze, waiting until she settled on her side with a soft sigh, curled up like a child. Her hand lay on top of the blankets. He had the strangest urge to reach over and take her fingers in his, but he suspected Mel would disapprove. Besides, he'd never been much of a hand holder, except with his young nephew.

"The two of you are close."

Mel smiled. "There are actually four cousins all together, and we Lowery women are more like sisters. I just happened to be the closest to Gallant Lake this week, visiting a designer in New York. I thought her plan was so crazy it might just work, but if it didn't, I wanted to be here for her." She looked at him. "*Did* it work?"

Good question. "Well, she pulled off getting the appointment, but..."

"She's good, Blake. You'd be damned lucky to have her." He glanced at the woman in his bed, and Mel frowned. "As your interior designer, I mean. Did she show you her portfolio? It should be in her bag..." Mel got up and searched through Amanda's leather bag, pulling out a spiral-bound notebook. "I think her photos of other projects are on her tablet, but here's her sketchbook." She handed it to him.

He opened the notebook absently. Hiring Lowery would be a colossally bad idea. He prided himself on making shrewd business decisions, and she couldn't possibly handle this... He blinked. He was looking at a drawing of Halcyon. But not the Halcyon he knew. Not even the Halcyon he saw in her original proposal. This Halcyon had life to it. And color. The living room had a sectional sofa facing the fireplace, with a flat screen on the wall. And a gaming console in the far corner. In a castle. Could he really do that? He flipped the page. This was the room that had intrigued him the most about her original proposal—the one he thought came from David Franklin. She wanted to turn the dining room into a huge home office. He'd need that if he ever decided to live here.

He'd never been one for settling down in one spot, but now that his nephew was going to be a part of his life, maybe it was time. And maybe this was the place. Amanda's drawings made the old castle look like a home.

Chapter Three

Amanda was having the weirdest medieval dream. She was in a massive, heavily carved mahogany bed. The room was large and round, with a marble fireplace. Ribbed cathedral ceilings arched so high that she couldn't see the top of them in the shadows. Tall windows were set into the walls, framed with heavy damask curtains.

A wingback chair was pulled up close to the bed, and a man was sitting there with his feet propped up on the mattress, watching silently. But this was no knight of the round table. Unless knights wore jeans and a T-shirt. Black hair curled down over his forehead.

Blake Randall.

This was no dream.

She sat up with a gasp, pulling the blanket with her. Peeking under it, she was relieved to see she was still fully clothed, sans shoes. Blake didn't react, watching as if he thought she might bolt. And she was seriously considering it. Her memory came back in fragments—collapsing in the living room, being carried up a winding staircase. She couldn't quite make sense of it all, but she didn't feel in danger.

"Where am I?"

Blake sat up and dropped his feet to the floor. Leaning forward, he rested his elbows on his knees, clasping his hands in front of him. His voice was soft and deep.

"You're in my suite at Halcyon."

"What time is it?"

"One o'clock."

"Does my cousin know I'm here, Mr. Randall? Does anyone?"

His mouth quirked into a smile.

"I didn't kidnap you. Mel just left to get some lunch." His smile deepened. "And I think we've been through enough together to be on a first-name basis. Call me Blake."

"Oh, my God—did you *carry* me up here?" she all but squeaked.

"It wasn't a big deal. There aren't that many furnished rooms in this place, so this was the logical choice."

Dr. Jackson kept telling her she had to deal with the past in order to move on, but they needed to rethink that plan if it was going to lead to impossible situations like this, with her waking up in some stranger's bed. Blake must think she was some pathetic, weak little creature, and that wasn't who she was. She wouldn't let it be.

"There's almost smoke coming from your ears from all that worrying you're doing. Relax."

"I should go…"

"Mel will be back soon. Get some more rest, and after lunch I promise I'll release you."

Her eyes narrowed at those last words, but his smile said he was joking. She settled back against the headboard, doing her best to ignore her burning humiliation and impending homelessness. Back to Kansas. Goodbye career.

"Hey…" Blake moved to sit on the edge of the bed. "What's wrong?" To her shock, he reached toward her face. She froze. He gently brushed her cheek with his thumb to sweep away a tear she hadn't realized she'd shed.

"What's *wrong*? I made a fool of myself today. I lied to get an interview with you, and then I had a panic attack in the middle of it. It's ridiculous. *I'm* ridiculous." She forced herself to stop talking. If she couldn't get her emotions under control, she deserved to go home to Mom. Maybe she'd find some nice job in a furniture store selling people plaid sofas.

"Come on, you had a panic attack. That's a physical condition that's out of your control." His hand dropped to rest on the mattress next to hers. "I'm just glad you're okay."

"Clearly, I'm a long way from okay. You've been kind, but I've taken enough of your time. I need to go."

"Stay…" His hand rested on hers, and he stared at it as if he was as surprised as she was.

They both heard Mel's footsteps, and quickly pulled their hands away from each other before she walked in. She looked back and forth between the two of them suspiciously before fixing her gaze on Amanda, who was wiping the last of the tears from her face.

"What happened?"

"I'm fine." Amanda's hands were shaking. She tucked them under her arms and tipped her head toward the box Mel carried. "I'm also starving."

Her cousin stared hard at her, then shrugged. "If you're up to it, there's plenty of food."

They ate together at the kitchen island, Blake and the two women. Mel was staring at him with sharp skepticism. And Amanda wouldn't look at him at all. He set her sketchbook on the marble counter.

"I looked at your drawings."

Amanda straightened. "You went through my *bag*? While I was unconscious?"

Mel started to stammer. "N-no, honey. I did. I wanted him to see your portfolio and the sketchbook was there, so…"

"Those were just dash-offs, not something I'd ever show to a client, Mel."

Blake spoke before Mel could respond.

"Amanda, you were right this morning. I *did* like your

original proposal. That's why I set up an appointment with someone who turned out to be you." He smiled at the flush of color on her cheeks. "And these sketches really make your ideas come to life." He opened the book. "I mean, a sectional in the living room? With a wide-screen TV? You seriously think that can work in a castle?"

"Sure. Victorian is all wrong for this place, and for you, I'm guessing." He grunted in agreement. He hated all the pink and green wallpaper. She nodded with a smile. "Halcyon's architecture is solid enough to support whatever style you want. I'd stick with the classics but give it a modern twist with some pops of color and fun accent pieces." She was in her element now. She might be young, but she knew her stuff. Her proposal had been highly detailed and professional. Even those dashed-off drawings were compelling.

"You really think this can be done?" He gestured to her sketch of the office.

"Of course. It's mostly cosmetic work. There's no actual construction, other than the bookcases in the office. The only reason the budget is so high is because of the sheer size of the place and massive amount of horrible wallpaper you have to remove."

"I need it completed before Christmas. Is that doable?" Nathan clearly had no interest in giving Zach a family Christmas, so it was going to be up to Blake. His chest grew tight. He'd never bought a Christmas decoration in his life, but he had to do *something* for the boy. Amanda was staring at him with wide eyes.

"What are you saying?"

"I'm saying you're hired." He set her sketchbook on the counter. He didn't believe in impulsive decisions, but this just felt right. "You've sold me on your vision. So tell me how long."

"Aaand this just turned into a business meeting," Mel laughed, "which is my cue to leave. I might still make my spa appointment after all." She gave Amanda a quick hug. "I knew you could do it, sweetie." Mel looked at Blake. "You've made a good decision."

"I haven't accepted the job yet." Amanda's chin jutted out in defiance.

Interesting. A few hours ago she'd been begging for it.

Mel laughed again. "You two don't need me to figure that out. Just don't overdo it after this morning. Got it?" That last question was for him.

"Got it." Satisfied, she left them alone.

Amanda looked a little shell-shocked, and he wanted to give her time to absorb her new job. But her silence dragged on so long he started having doubts. He flipped through the sketchbook again.

"Are you suggesting painting the wrought-iron chandeliers *orange*? That's not a pop of color, it's… I don't know… an explosion?"

"It's not orange, it's paprika." She sounded prim and defensive. "It's a spice color. It brings a touch of fun and whimsy to the space. This should be a home where you feel free to kick off your shoes and relax without feeling guilty about it."

"I doubt *fun* and *whimsical* are words people normally associate with me."

"So surprise them."

He looked back at the drawings. "*You've* surprised *me.* Are you taking the job?"

She hesitated. "Don't hire me out of pity, Blake. I don't want your charity."

He gave her a steely glare that usually had his employees quaking in their shoes. She blinked, but didn't look away when he spoke. "I run a billion-dollar business. I don't make decisions based on pity. You're a designer out of work. I'm looking to hire a designer. Do you want the job or not?"

Her willingness to walk away from a job she needed

and obviously wanted surprised him. Finally she sighed and pushed her plate away "Let's take another look together and discuss it."

"I promised Mel we wouldn't over— "

"I'm not talking about taking a grand tour. But this kitchen is too modern—it's an add-on, right?" He nodded. The 1990s kitchen was efficient, but generic. Amanda grimaced. "I can't feel the house in here."

Blake had no clue what that meant, but he followed her into the main hall. She rested her hand on the mantel and smiled a secret little smile that made his pulse quicken.

"This was once a home so full of love." She looked up at him through long lashes. "Do you know its history?"

"Yes. The stories are full of romance and tragedy—"

"Tell me the stories." Her gentle smile wasn't a secret this time. It was aimed at *him*, and it caused him to stutter.

"T-tell you what?"

"Tell me the stories of Halcyon. Knowing the history of a home helps me get a feel for its personality."

He shook his head. He wasn't a storyteller. No one had read him fairy tales as a kid. No one had read him anything. Even the nannies were too busy for such frivolity. He wondered if Zach liked stories. Had Tiffany used to read to her son? "There are plenty of people around who know the history better than I do. I just wanted the land, not the legend."

"There's a *legend*? Now you have to tell me!"

He leaned against the mantel and racked his brain for the history of Halcyon. He'd been disgusted with the whole stupid story right up until the moment Amanda Lowery fell in love with it.

"The house was built in the late 1800s by a wealthy banker from New York named Otis Pendleton. His young wife, Madeleine, fell ill, and they thought the country air might cure her. She got better, and apparently Otis had money to burn, so he built her a castle here. He stayed in the city during the week and came here on weekends to see her and the kids."

Amanda walked over to the ebony staircase and sat on the steps. He followed her.

"Are you tired? We can do this another time..."

She waved her hand in dismissal. "I'm fine, just taking it all in. Finish the story." He stared at her, and she gestured for him to get going. She was a bossy little thing when she wasn't a nervous wreck. He sat on the stairs below her, stretching his legs out in front of him.

"Pendleton lost everything in the stock market crash in the twenties. He took his own life, jumping out the window of his twentieth-floor Manhattan office." Amanda gasped. "Some people insist his brother pushed him. I guess there was bad blood there. The children were sure Otis never would have left Madeleine alone, because they were so much in love."

Amanda sighed wistfully, looking around the empty hall. He had a sneaking suspicion she wasn't seeing an empty room. She was picturing it as the Pendletons' home. He wasn't surprised she was a romantic. He was only surprised that he suddenly felt a bit of a romantic himself just telling her.

"Madeleine was grief stricken and took to her bed upstairs. She died before they could evict her and auction off the house. Supposedly she haunts the place."

"It's *haunted*? Have you seen her?"

He rolled his eyes. "Have I seen Madeleine Pendleton walking around Halcyon? Uh, no."

Amanda looked over her shoulder and up the winding staircase. He knew she was hoping to see some ghostly apparition, but there was nothing to suggest the place was actually haunted. Well...nothing other than some creaky stairs at night and the odd scent of roses in the solarium.

"What happened after Madeleine died?"

"Halcyon's been a little of everything—a boardinghouse, a motel…rumor has it, it was a brothel for a few years. It was deserted for a long time. A young couple with more money than good sense bought it back in the nineties and poured their penny stock fortune into it, trying to make it into a bed-and-breakfast." He glanced up. She was hanging on every word. "They're the ones that added the kitchen and the elevator. But there wasn't enough income to cover all the work they did. They closed it up ten years ago, and I bought it last year." It was surprising how comfortable it was to sit here and talk with her. He looked up at the wood ceilings, feeling more affection for the house than he'd felt since he'd bought it. "Most buildings fall into disrepair very quickly when empty, especially old ones, but this one held up surprisingly well."

"You've told me the stories, but what's the legend?"

He groaned. "Legend has it that Madeleine won't be happy until the place is a private home again, and that's why no business has survived here. I guess that means you're right. It wouldn't be a good idea to put offices in here."

She smiled, but it faded quickly at his next question.

"Are you taking the job?"

"I don't know, Blake. It's a bit overwhelming."

"You don't think you're capable of a project like this?"

She sat up sharply. "Of *course* I'm capable. I specialize in period homes. I can handle this." She gestured around her.

Blake gave her a triumphant grin.

"You *are* taking the job. And you can do it by Christmas?" It was suddenly imperative that he give Zach a happy Christmas this year to erase the memory of the last one.

"It's a lot of work to get done in a few months."

"You've convinced me this place can be a home, and I happen to need one. By Christmas."

Her forehead furrowed. "You don't have a home?"

"I use the owner suites at whatever resort I'm at."

"How many resorts do you own?"

He shrugged. "Five. You still haven't answered my question. Can you have it done by the holidays?"

"Some of the furniture will need to be ordered and may not be here in time..." Amanda looked around, and he could tell she was calculating in her head. It was a hot look on her. *Damn it.* He stood and moved away. Where the hell did *that* thought come from?

Her face scrunched, then relaxed, as if coming to a conclusion she approved of. "With enough skilled people, I could probably get most of the work done in time. I'll need a place to live..."

"If you want to commute from the city, I can send a car for you."

"Umm... I'm actually...between apartments right now. It would be easier to find a rental here in town."

He kicked himself. He forgot Mel had told him Amanda was losing her apartment.

"Stay here at the house."

He probably should have thought that idea through before saying it out loud.

"What?" She stood, her gaze darting around the empty hall. "Here? No."

"Look, it's a big place. There's a nice suite upstairs with a balcony. I'm leaving for Hawaii and Bali in mid-September—I won't even be here part of the time. I'd give you a room down at the resort, but September's probably booked solid for leaf season." He could tell she was considering it. "You can order your meals from the resort, of course. We'll configure lodging and meals as part of the package. I'll have Julie make all the arrangements. Her brother's a contractor, and he's done good work at the resort and around town. Bobby can handle what you're planning to do, and he can find workers locally. And don't worry about being alone here. The security system is excellent…" He was practically begging, and he had no clue why. He just knew he wanted her to say yes. She stared at him for a long moment, then nodded, all business.

"I'll need a week or two to pack my things and get settled. I'll need to meet with the contractor as soon as possible so we can set up a schedule."

"I'll call Bobby in the morning to set up a meeting."

He wasn't prepared for her next question.

"You don't even like this place, so why spend the money? Why the rush to be ready for Christmas?"

He started to answer, but emotion tangled up his words and kept them from coming out. He looked up at the high ceilings and blew out a deep breath.

"I have a nephew. He's my responsibility now that my sister is dead." He ignored her small sound of sympathy. "Being a nomad worked for me before, but that needs to change. I'd never considered this place an option before you showed up. It's close enough to the city to be workable for me. And Zach…well, a boy should like living in a castle, right?"

She started to laugh, then apparently realized he was serious. Yeah, he was damned serious. He had no clue what a ten-year-old boy liked.

"Blake, every child in the world would *love* to live in a castle." She patted his arm affectionately. "I'll make sure he loves this one when I'm done with it."

They exchanged business cards and cell phone numbers, then Blake called the resort and had someone pick her up so she wouldn't have to walk. He watched her go down the front steps. Her long blond curls swayed in counter rhythm to her hips. Damn, she was the real deal. Talented. Creative. And drop-dead sexy.

She was working for him now. Her voice and face

changed when she talked about design work. She lost her nervousness. And she'd be living in his house. He closed his eyes and grimaced. What the hell had he just done? He may have just created his very own hell here at Halcyon.

The sooner he was off to Hawaii, the better.

Chapter Four

When Amanda walked into the restaurant at the Gallant Lake Resort two weeks later, she could barely stay on her feet. Every muscle ached from packing up the apartment she'd shared with two other women. Doubts about her decision to take this job—to *move* here—kept her awake every night. Most of her belongings were now packed into a storage unit in the city. It was depressing to see how little space her entire life took up. And now she had to meet her general contractor tonight over dinner.

She'd settled into Halcyon that morning, unpacking her clothes and the handful of personal things she'd brought with her. The sunny yellow suite on the third floor would be her home for the next few months. An odd flutter of déjà vu had tickled up her spine when she stepped out onto the long stone balcony outside her room. But she hadn't felt afraid. If anything, the familiarity of it all made her feel more relaxed. And the room did have a spectacular view.

At first, she'd wondered why Blake Randall put her in the room right next to his. But after walking through the house, she realized there weren't many options, since so few of the rooms were furnished. The entire second floor was vacant. And the other tower room on the third floor clearly belonged to the young nephew he'd mentioned, since the bed was covered with teddy bears. A key to the house had been delivered to her apartment a few days ago, along with a cryptic handwritten note.

*I won't be there to help you get settled, but two of
my employees from the resort will be waiting at the
house on Wednesday to assist with the move. I have
a meeting in Vegas, but I should be back Wednesday
night. Julie and Bobby will expect you to meet them
for dinner at seven at Galantè to discuss logistics.
Blake.*

It was hard to believe the note had been written by the
same guy who'd brushed a tear from her cheek, but maybe
that version of Blake Randall was the exception, not the
rule. He was now her client, so it made sense he wanted
to keep things professional. And yet he chose to put her in
the suite next to his. She was too tired to sort out her feelings about that.

Galantè was the formal dining venue at the resort, with
a wall of windows overlooking Gallant Lake. It was mid-
September, and the lake was ablaze with the reflected colors from the trees surrounding it as the sun set. Amanda
glanced down at her tailored navy blue dress and matching pumps, thankful for the wardrobe she'd acquired back
when she was earning a steady paycheck. She was here
for a business dinner, and she could do this. Her exhaustion rolled off her shoulders as her adrenaline amped up.
The renovation at Halcyon would be the perfect project to
begin her own design firm.

Julie Brown, the assistant manager, waved from a table
near the windows. Julie and her brother, Bobby, weren't
twins, but they could have been with the similarities in their
looks and personalities. Both had thick brown hair, hazel
eyes, and warm smiles. Julie's hair was cut short in a lay-
ered bob. Bobby's hair was longer than his sister's, sweeping across his forehead and brushing his shoulders. They
had the same teasing sense of humor, and they laughed
often and easily.

Amanda leaned back in her seat after dinner, feeling satisfied. Not just about the food, but also about the design project. Bobby was more than qualified to tackle what needed to be done at Halcyon. He'd just finished building a custom home for a client, and he didn't have another job lined up, so his crew could start immediately.

Julie cleared her throat and folded her napkin carefully on her empty dessert plate. "Mr. Randall told me you're staying at Halcyon, even while he's gone." Julie shook her head. "You're braver than me, that's for sure. Anyway, I've made arrangements for housekeeping to go up there daily to take care of the living quarters and you can eat all your meals here at the resort."

"I don't need housekeeping, Julie. I can clean up after myself, and there's an old washer and dryer there I can use for my laundry. And I actually love to cook, so I'll feed myself…" Her voice faded when she saw Julie's smile disappear.

"Mr. Randall insisted on the housekeeping and meals. I don't think he'll be happy if you don't accept it."

Amanda rolled her eyes. She didn't want Julie to be in trouble with Blake. "Fine. Send housekeeping up twice a week to do the general stuff. But I'm washing my own clothes and I want to be able to cook. Is there a grocery store near here?"

"There's one on the other side of the village, but our chef can order whatever you want from his suppliers. Mr. Randall won't want you paying for groceries."

"Well, Mr. Randall isn't always going to get what he wants." The last thing Amanda needed was some man trying to take over her life. It was time to take on that role for herself. "I'm more self-sufficient than you might think based on seeing me pass out a couple weeks ago." Julie probably thought of Amanda as some frail thing. But she was certainly capable of driving to the store. Except for one problem. Keeping a car in New York City was ridiculously expensive, so she'd given hers up years ago. "Is there a vehicle I can use until I figure out my car situation?"

"The resort has a minivan…"

"Nonsense." Blake Randall's deep voice made Amanda sit straighter. He slid into the seat next to her. "Amanda can drive one of my cars or use the limo."

Julie slipped immediately into her professional persona. "Of course, Mr. Randall."

Amanda tried to picture herself going to the little grocery store in Gallant Lake in a limousine. Hopefully he had a vehicle she'd feel comfortable driving, because the limo idea wasn't going to work.

He shook Bobby's hand. "I'm sorry I couldn't be here for dinner. Have you made all the arrangements you need?"

Bobby's head nodded in acknowledgment. "Yes, Mr. Randall. I'll start ordering supplies tomorrow, and we'll set up next week to start stripping the walls. I grew up in Gallant Lake and I've always wanted to get inside that old house, so I'm really excited about this job."

They talked about the plans for Halcyon over coffee. Blake hardly looked Amanda's way as he walked her back to the castle when they were done. His stride was quick and tense, and she had to scramble in her heels to keep up. They'd hardly spoken since agreeing to this arrangement, and she wondered if he was having regrets now that she was here. Or maybe he was always this uptight. She tried not to sound out of breath.

"Is there anything you want to discuss?"

"No. Why?" He didn't even glance at her, and her discomfort grew.

"You seem…um…tense. If you'd be more comfortable with me staying somewhere else…"

"Do you *want* to stay somewhere else? Are you nervous about staying at Halcyon?"

"No, not at all." They walked up the back steps to the veranda, and the house glowed in the soft twilight. Nothing scared her about this house. "But I don't want to intrude on your life here."

He looked out to the lake, shoving his hands in his pockets. "I don't have a life here, Amanda. I'm a very busy man, and you're about to be a very busy woman with this project, so we won't be bothering each other much."

"I just don't want to be one of those annoying houseguests who gets underfoot."

His brows lowered. "You're not a houseguest. We're not roommates. You're an employee who happens to be using a room in a property I own. You're on your own here. You said you'd be okay with that."

"I *am* fine with it."

"Good."

"Fine."

He turned toward the house, effectively dismissing her. She'd upheaved her entire life to come here, and the exhaustion and uncertainty caught up with her, coming out of her mouth in annoyance.

"You know, for someone in the hospitality business, you can be downright *in*hospitable, Blake."

He stopped, then slowly turned back to face her. His dark eyes narrowed, and she braced herself. He was already having regrets, and now he was going to fire her. Where the hell would she go?

His glower lasted another moment, then he shook his head and…laughed. It was a soft chuckle, more at himself than anything. He squinted and looked at the darkening lake behind her, then met her eyes and smiled. Holy hotness, he had a great smile.

"I've never thought of it that way, but you're right. I *was* being pretty inhospitable, wasn't I? Good for you for calling me out on it. Most people don't." He rolled his shoulders and rubbed the back of his neck. "I'm sorry. It was a long flight from Vegas, capped off with another phone argument with my father. I didn't mean to take it out on you."

"You don't get along with your dad?"

He shrugged and frowned. "Never have. Did you get settled in your suite today? Do you need anything?"

She recognized the rapid subject change as deflection. She was good at that, too, and she decided to let him get away with it. He didn't owe her any explanations about his family life.

"The room is lovely, and I'm all unpacked. I'm going to head back into the city tomorrow to check out some design centers and look at furniture. If I can snag a few floor samples, I can save us some time on the remodel." She figured she could ask Julie to drop her off at the train station two towns over.

He shrugged absently. His mind wasn't on the remodel. Maybe he was still dwelling on the fight with his father. Or his nephew. Whom she hadn't met yet.

"Where is your nephew living?" she asked. "With your father?"

Blake snorted. "Definitely not. Zachary was with my brother's family for the summer, but he's at boarding school now."

"Boarding school? How old is he?" She didn't even know boarding school was still a thing, and there were teddy bears in the boy's bedroom.

"He just turned ten."

"*Ten?* And you're sending him off to boarding school? Why can't he go to school here in Gallant Lake?"

He laughed again, but there was no warmth to it. "To public school? I don't think so. Beakman Academy is in Connecticut, so he's not that far away. With my travel schedule, it's the best place for him."

"You make it sound like you're boarding a dog, not a little boy."

His face hardened. "Do you always speak your mind about things that don't concern you?"

She gulped hard, but stood her ground. "Just a minute ago you were praising my ability to call you out."

His brow arched, and her heart skipped. "You called me out on my treatment of *you*. My nephew's education has nothing to do with you." He glanced at his watch. "I have a conference call in a few minutes with the West Coast. I'll take it in my room. Good night, Amanda."

And this time, he really did dismiss her, walking into the house without another glance. She blew out the breath she didn't know she'd been holding and looked toward the lake. They were going to have to figure out how to live under the same roof and maintain personal boundaries. She'd obviously crossed his. His nephew, poor kid, was off-limits for conversation. Duly noted.

After spending Thursday furniture shopping in the city, Amanda met Julie for breakfast Friday morning. Blake seemed to spend most of his time in his office at the resort, getting ready for his trip to his other resorts. Julie introduced Amanda to the resort's chef. Dario Manzetti was short, round and energetic, and she liked him immediately. The charming Italian man referred to her as his little *bambolina* and kissed both her cheeks when they met. He had a machine-gun laugh that filled the large kitchen, and she couldn't help but laugh right along with him. His hands flew through the air in wild gestures with every word he spoke, and she wondered how he was able to cook and talk if his hands were this integral to communicating.

She worried he might be offended that she preferred to do her own cooking, but Dario was delighted. He agreed to order whatever supplies she needed, and smiled in approval when she wrote out her list of basic staples for the Halcyon kitchen.

That night, Blake surprised her with Chinese takeout from the village to share for dinner. They sat at the kitchen island and shared a bottle of wine as she outlined her and Bobby's revised plans for the house from their meeting that afternoon. The conversation was strictly business, but oddly comfortable. There was something about Blake, when he wasn't distracted and cranky, that calmed her perpetual undercurrent of tension.

The scaffolding went up the following week, with the marble floors covered with heavy canvas drop cloths. Halcyon was officially a construction zone. Blake left for the city early that morning, so he'd missed most of the noise and chaos. The surprise on his face when he returned that evening told her that, like many clients, he hadn't grasped how all-consuming this project was going to be. She bit back a grin as he walked carefully around the ladders and supplies. It was a good thing he'd be gone for a while on that business trip because it was only going to get worse.

She poured two glasses of wine and walked out to meet him in the main hall. He was staring up at the scaffolding with a frown.

"Every good project starts like this, Blake." She handed him a glass. "I know it seems overwhelming, but I promise I know what I'm doing."

"I'm sure you do." His words were more confident than his expression.

"Look, I know you're leaving Friday…" Saying those words out loud stung more than she expected. They hadn't spent a lot of time together. They'd shared a few meals, although there was never any cooking involved—he ordered food from the resort's restaurant or got takeout. For breakfast, he'd just grab a bagel and leave her lingering over her much-needed morning coffee. They'd never discussed anything too personal but still, the conversations flowed easily enough. She cleared her throat and smiled up at him.

"I'd like to treat you to a home-cooked dinner here tomorrow night. No takeout." His eyes widened in surprise, so she rushed to explain. "I want to do something to show my appreciation for…well, for everything. The job, certainly, but also for…being so generous. You know…after I lied and fainted and all that…"

He shook his head. "That's not necessary, Amanda."

"It is for me."

He finally shrugged, looking away to take in the construction site again.

"Will we be dining on a table made from plywood and scaffolding?"

"No!" She laughed and he glanced back at her, smiling warmly. That smile caused her to stutter a little. Must. Stay. Professional. "The—the solarium is dusty, but it's clutter-free right now, and there's a small table out there. I think I can make it work for dinner. Is six okay?"

"You really don't have to—"

"I want to, Blake. It's just dinner."

If it was just dinner, why did it feel like it might be something more? She shook herself mentally as Blake walked away. It *was* just dinner. It had to be. He was her client and she was a complete professional.

Blake stared at the reports spread across the desk in his office Thursday afternoon. He'd just finished a conference call with the construction crew in Bali. It was a good thing he'd be there soon, because things were moving far too slowly.

As usual, his thoughts drifted to Amanda. He couldn't seem to escape her this week. For a petite little package, that woman managed to be *everywhere*. He saw her in the mornings, all sleepy eyed and husky voiced until she had her second cup of coffee. He'd watched her with Bobby and the workers. She kept her distance physically, but she was smart and in charge, and they knew it. She got along well with Bobby, and they spent a lot of time discussing plans. Blake frowned. A *lot* of time.

He couldn't even escape her at the resort, where she and Julie had lunch together every day. He was glad the two women were friends so Amanda wouldn't be alone while he was traveling. But to turn around in the middle of the day and see her leaning against the front desk, her blond hair falling over her shoulder, laughing with Julie over some girlie thing…well, it made something twist in his gut.

He was doing his best to keep things strictly business with her. He tried not to allow their conversations to drift to anything other than the Halcyon project. Or, at most, to safe topics like movies and stuff. Nothing personal. It was the only way for him to keep that fortress around his heart standing solid. He did not want to get involved with her. Well, he *did* want to, but he wasn't going to. It was bound to end just as badly as every other relationship he'd ever had, and she was working for him. That was a level of messiness he wanted nothing to do with.

He frowned at the investment report he was supposed to be reviewing, then tossed it down and stood, and walked to the windows overlooking the lake. His mind went back to Amanda laughing with Bobby this morning. Bobby was single. He seemed like a good guy. His sister was Amanda's new best friend. Was Bobby interested in Amanda? Would he ask her out while Blake was traveling? Would she say yes? Would he come back home in a month to find that he'd lost her?

He cursed out loud in the empty office.

She wasn't his to lose! He tried to remember that, but it got tougher every day he spent with her at Halcyon. Maybe he should have left for Hawaii on Monday. He picked up the report, then threw it down on the desk a second time. Maybe he should walk up to Halcyon to see what she was doing.

He found her in the living room. Talking with Bobby. His jaw tightened. She gestured animatedly at the wall of windows and doors facing the veranda. When Bobby glanced in his direction, she turned midsentence to face him. And nearly gave him a heart attack. She was wearing skintight jeans and a snug blue top that matched her eyes, with her hair pulled up in a long ponytail that swung as she moved. Her clothes were dusty and a sheen of sweat glistened on her forehead. She wore no makeup, and she had a smudge of dirt on one cheek. He didn't think he'd ever seen anything more beautiful.

He barely registered that there were two other men in the room besides Bobby, up on ladders doing...something. He walked straight to her as if she was pulling him in. She was relaxed. Happy. Was it the job giving her more confidence? The house? Or was she finally becoming comfortable with him?

"Bobby and I were just discussing the window treatments. There's a company that makes draperies out of sails—they're actual used sails from boats. They're stitched together and sometimes there's a random big number or letter on them. They're so cool, and they'd be perfect for this wall, with the water in the background. When the windows are open they'll move with the breeze. The look will be so—" She stopped and sighed. "You can't picture it at all, can you?"

No. He couldn't. But he loved that she could. "You're the one with the vision."

"You'll love it. I promise."

A long ringlet of blond hair fell across her face. Without thinking, Blake reached out to push it behind her ear. Her teasing smile faded and her eyes grew wide. He forgot what they were talking about. He forgot that anyone else was in the room. He forgot everything except how beautiful she was. She swallowed hard and stepped back. He realized then that his fingertips had been resting on the side of her neck, just behind her ear. He cleared his throat and dropped his hand.

Her mouth quirked up into a half grin, then it faded. She was nervous. "Dinner's at six. I need to start getting ready."

With that, she walked away. Her jeans were tight, and her top was tighter. And something on him was a little tighter than normal, too.

He turned to look at the lake, trying to figure out how the hell he was going to be able to have dinner alone with her tonight. This wasn't take-out food at the kitchen island. It was a sit-down meal together. He wasn't sure he could come up with enough questions about the renovation to fill an entire dinner with business talk, and over the past week or so they'd covered every movie of the past century. Maybe he should invent some excuse to skip it. But the meal was already cooking—he could smell it. He was just going to have to control his attraction to his interior designer. Surely he was man enough to manage that.

Chapter Five

Amanda stepped back to admire her work. The beat-up old table was pretty now that it was covered with a crisp white tablecloth she'd borrowed from the resort. Blake mentioned one night over Chinese food that he hardly ever went into the solarium, and she wanted to show him how lovely the room could be as a casual dining and conversation area. The curved walls were lined with windows, with ornate white iron accents tracing up the high ceiling that radiated out from the stone walls of the main house. Tiny blue, green, yellow and white tiles covered the floor in a mosaic design. The room was in desperate need of cleaning and a coat of paint, but it was cozy and always seemed to smell of roses.

The kitchen was boring, but large and nice to work in. Sure, the oven was temperamental and utensils were sparse, but she enjoyed the challenge. She'd plugged her phone into a minispeaker, and her playlist was at full volume. She'd showered and changed earlier, and her long blue skirt swirled around her ankles as she moved. The pork chops were almost done, and a freshly made blueberry cobbler sat on the counter. If there was one thing she'd learned growing up in the heart of the Midwest, it was how to cook.

Bruno Mars was singing about all that funk. She tore up a head of fresh romaine for a Caesar salad, humming along to the music and dancing her way around the island. She was still singing when she grabbed the salad bowl to take to the table. She spun around and let out a squeal of surprise.

Blake was leaning against the doorway to the kitchen, arms crossed, watching her with obvious amusement. The glass bowl bobbled in her arms, and he jumped forward and took it from her.

"You were having such a good time that I didn't want to interrupt your performance." He was flashing her that smile that always melted her. "Are you planning on being my singing waitress tonight? If so, I'm not sure Mr. Mars is period authentic for Halcyon."

"A singing *chef* would be more accurate, I think. And I like Bruno." She turned to the oven to check the meal, ignoring his snort of laughter behind her. She opened the oven door and started muttering. "Damn it. This thing just doesn't want to stay lit." She turned the knobs back and forth a few times, and the pilot light started clicking before the oven came back on with a soft whooshing sound. "There we go."

When she turned back to Blake, he was staring at her with some combination of amazement and confusion.

"You're cooking dinner?"

"Yes." She spoke to him as if she was talking to a small child.

"You cooked it from scratch? It's not Dario's food?"

She straightened. Did he think she wasn't capable of cooking a meal?

"Well, I didn't go out and kill the pig, but yes, I cooked everything from scratch. Including dessert." She gestured to the blueberry cobbler sitting on the marble counter. "It's not that unusual for women to know how to cook, you know."

He looked at the dessert as if he'd just discovered a Rembrandt masterpiece sitting in his kitchen.

"I've never had a woman cook dinner for me before."

Her mouth dropped open. "Never? Not even your mother?"

He snorted and shook his head. "*Especially* not my mother. No woman has cooked for me unless she was paid to. My parents had staff, and now I always stay at my resorts, where *I* have staff. And the ladies in my life have all been firm supporters of restaurants and room service."

Her cheeks flamed. He was rich and handsome, and probably had plenty of "ladies" available to him. But she didn't need to hear about them.

He was still holding the salad bowl. "What would you like me to do with this?"

She rolled her eyes. Was he really this inept at having a simple meal at home?

"Unless you're planning to eat straight from the bowl, I'd suggest you set it on the dining table." His eyes narrowed at her sarcasm. "We're eating out in the solarium, if I can keep this damned stove running. Do you think you can handle pouring two glasses of wine for us? I've already opened it, so you don't have to be nervous about learning any other new skills." She nodded toward the bottle at the end of the island.

"You may want to stow that sharp tongue of yours, young lady. I'm not usually fond of being mocked." He was grinning again, playing along. She hadn't seen much of the playful side of Blake Randall. She liked it.

He walked out of the kitchen with the salad, then came back to pour the wine while she removed dinner from the oven. He watched in apparent fascination as she arranged the food on their plates and turned toward the solarium. She lifted her chin toward the wineglasses, and he obediently picked them up and followed her to the table.

Conversation flowed easily over dinner. They talked about the legends surrounding Halcyon and his fight with the locals over his plans to demolish the building and the neighboring resort. She whispered a quiet prayer of thanks to the devoted citizens of Gallant Lake who weren't afraid to stand up to Blake and his wealth. They'd saved this wonderful house.

Blake's deep voice interrupted her rambling thoughts. "Hey, where'd you go?"

"Hmm? Oh, sorry." She pushed her empty dessert plate away. "You may not want to hear this, but I'm glad the house was saved."

His eyes went wide. "Are you saying you're happy I lost in court?"

"Yes, actually, I am. They preserved an important part of Gallant Lake's history."

"And do you support their fight against my casino, as well?"

She couldn't lie to the man.

"Yes."

He sat back in his chair and stared at her. "You continually manage to surprise me, Amanda. Your honesty is refreshing." The corner of his mouth twitched. "Even when it's irritating."

"Yeah, well, my therapist says honesty is always—" she held her fingers up in air quotes "—the 'fastest way through a problem' and I'm trying to follow her lead." She frowned. She couldn't believe she just quoted Dr. Jackson to him. She never talked about her therapy. She ran her fingers up and down the stem of her wineglass absently, wondering if it was the alcohol or the company that had her talking so freely.

"Tell me about what happened to you this summer."

Her head snapped up and she stared at Blake in surprise. "Wh-what do you mean?"

They stared at each other in silence. He reached for the wine bottle and refilled her glass. And waited. Damn Mel and her chatty morning with Blake the day Amanda fainted. She must have spilled more than she'd admitted to. Amanda took a deep breath and ignored her pounding pulse.

"It all started when I lost my job in May." The memory still galled her. She never should have trusted David. "It was one of the hottest new firms in Manhattan, and I was thrilled to be part of it." Until she'd discovered what David had done. How he'd used her. She did her best to appear nonchalant. "And then everything went to hell."

"Were you and David Franklin *together*?"

"Ew. No." Her face twisted. "But not for lack of trying on his part. He was more interested in my design ideas than me, though. He was taking credit for my work with the clients." David stole the one thing from her that she truly loved—her work. "He used photos of my work in his personal portfolio. Not as an associate's work, but as his own. I found out he'd done the same thing with other designers. Hadn't had an original idea for years. Instead of walking away, I confronted him."

"Good for you." Blake's voice was warm with admiration.

"Well, it didn't turn out very good. I'd been writing a proposal for a new client—a huge apartment in a historic building, overlooking Central Park. After I told David I knew what he was doing, he told my client I'd been caught overbilling another account. She refused to work with me." Amanda took a deep breath, still feeling the burning shame of that afternoon. "I went back to the office and found my things in a box. But they forgot to lock me out of the email server. That's how I managed to see your RFP for Halcyon." He smiled at that, and she couldn't help but return it. That rare burst of unethical behavior had worked out pretty well for her. And it served David right. "I had a small nest egg saved, but not enough to last long in New York. David started spreading all kinds of lies to destroy my credibility, just in case I decided to tell someone what he'd done. I couldn't get hired." Her eyes fell to where her fingers toyed with her wineglass. She hadn't taken a sip since he refilled it.

She didn't intend to tell Blake about what came next.

She really didn't. He'd never know the difference. What she'd already told him was surely bad enough to qualify as a Truly Terrible Summer.

He cleared his throat and she looked up as he started to speak.

"Franklin is a jackass. I'm sor—"

"I'm not finished." She inhaled sharply after she said that. Of course she was finished. She wasn't going to tell him about that night. *Stop talking!*

"I went out with some former coworkers in July." Oh, hell, that was *her* mouth that just blurted out those words. Blake's eyes widened, but he didn't speak. "It was late and I decided to walk home so I could think things through. And I was…attacked."

Blake had started to raise the wineglass to his lips, but now he set it back down on the table very slowly, as if he was afraid of shattering it. His eyes grew dark and intense as he listened.

"I was so deep in my own self-pity that I forgot to pay attention to my surroundings. A guy grabbed me from behind and forced me into a narrow alley. He reeked of cigarette smoke…" Her entire body shuddered at the memory. For the second time in her life she'd been helpless against an attacker. "He shoved me up against the wall and grabbed…" Her voice trailed off and Blake spoke, his voice gruff with emotion.

"You don't have to tell me any more."

She waved her hand at him in dismissal. "There's not much more to tell. I struggled. He put a knife to my throat and told me he'd kill me if I didn't do what he said."

Blake blinked, then blinked again. Son. Of. A. *Bitch*.

Amanda took a ragged breath and finished quickly. "A short-order cook stepped into the alley right then to smoke a cigarette, and he came running at the guy when he saw what was happening. The man took off. That cook saved my life." She tried to grin again, but couldn't hold it. "I guess my terrible summer could have been worse. It could have been my *last* summer."

She lifted her glass in a mock toast, but he didn't touch his. He couldn't shake the image of her body thrown against an alley wall. Thank God for that cook. This all happened in the past few months, and she was still standing strong. This woman was tough as nails.

"I'm sorry you had to go through any of that." They stared at each other in silence. The color that had drained from her face when she spoke about the assault returned now, turning her cheeks bright pink.

He could see her sweeping it all away in her mind. Tucking it in some safe dark place so she could go on with her life. She finally pulled her shoulders back and met his gaze. Yep. Tough as nails.

"I've made it to September—almost October now. Hopefully this job will be the start of a much better autumn. I'm looking forward to bringing Halcyon back to life." She stood and started picking up the dishes. "Now come help me clean up."

She needed to close the door on the conversation, and he was more than happy to help her do that. But cleaning up?

"I have staff for that, Amanda."

She rolled her eyes. She did that a lot. Then she laughed. At him. She seemed to do that a lot, too. And damned if he didn't like the way it made him feel.

"Oh, for God's sake, Blake, pick up the dishes and help me clean the kitchen. Housekeeping is only coming up twice a week, and I'm not leaving them my dirty dishes. Of course, if the dishwasher is as reliable as the stove, we may both end up with dishpan hands." She looked over her shoulder at him with a bright smile. And like an obedient little puppy, he found himself piling dirty dishes together and following her into the kitchen.

He set a stack of dishes and glasses on top of the cooking pan in the sink when Amanda reached out to stop him.

"What are you doing? You can't wash that fine crystal with the pots and pans! Have you *really* never washed dishes before?"

He stared at her in consternation. It never occurred to him that dish washing was a critical life skill he was lacking. Why did he feel embarrassed to admit to her that he was absolutely clueless in the kitchen?

"Um… I…didn't know…"

Her blue eyes went wide, sparkling with humor.

"Wow. I honestly thought you were exaggerating about no one ever cooking for you. But you really don't know anything about how a kitchen operates, do you?" She quickly pulled the greasy cooking pans out of the sink, replacing them with the dinner dishes. She set the crystal glasses aside while she filled the sink with soap and water. "You were born into a wealthy family?"

He turned and took a towel from the oven door. Surely he could dry a few dishes without embarrassing himself. When he turned back to face her, his breath caught in his chest. Her hair was falling loose tonight, curls rolling down her back. Her sweater matched her eyes. They were standing close enough that he could smell her spicy perfume. She looked up at him expectantly, but he was too busy getting lost in those eyes.

"Blake?"

"Hmm? What?" He took a step back in an attempt to regain his equilibrium.

"You came from a wealthy family?"

He grimaced. Talking about his family was a surefire way to cool his libido.

"Wealthy? Yes—the proverbial silver spoon. My father

comes from a long line of successful investors. My mother's Texas family made, then lost, a ton of oil money. She married my father because he could keep her in the lifestyle she felt entitled to. Mother thought manual labor was vulgar."

And then she'd decided motherhood was equally vulgar, but he didn't say that out loud. He glanced at Amanda, up to her elbows in soapsuds, and grinned. She was nothing at all like his mother. "No offense," he added.

She snorted. "None taken. My middle-class Midwestern family felt manual labor was somewhere akin to godliness. I've been washing dishes since I was five."

"I guess you had the quintessential perfect childhood, eh?"

Her mouth trembled slightly. "Not exactly perfect."

"Let me guess—you lived in a pretty little house on a tree-lined street with sidewalks and picket fences. Your happy mom and dad had two-point-four children and a dog. You were an all-American girl with long blond pigtails. I bet you were even a cheerleader in high school, the one all the boys chased."

A dinner plate started to slip from her hands, but she caught it before it hit the side of the sink.

"Amanda?"

The color drained from her face. He forced himself to stand still, cursing under his breath when he noticed how badly her hands were trembling. What just happened? He wanted to reach for her, but he had a feeling touching her would be the wrong thing to do.

She took a deep breath, putting that artificial smile on her face. Her overly musical voice sounded forced. "You only got the neighborhood right. I'm an only child. My father died at Christmas when I was six. My stepdad didn't allow pets, so there was no dog. And I *hated* high school." The last words were said with unusual force.

They fell into an awkward silence. The atmosphere in

the room snapped with electricity. Amanda worked at a frantic pace and flinched every time he brushed against her. He felt responsible for making her this way, but he didn't know what the hell he'd done. His jaw tightened. He didn't like problems he couldn't fix. He had to figure out how to fix this.

She hadn't been this uptight when she'd talked about everything that happened all summer. Why was she freaking out *now*, talking about her childhood? There were a lot of possible answers to that question, and none of them were good. She reached past him for a large roasting pan. It slipped out of her fingers and dropped with a loud clatter against the stone counter. She let out a squeal of fright.

Okay, enough was enough. The woman was going to give herself a heart attack at this rate. He set his hands lightly on her shoulders, being careful not to hold her too tightly, just enough to stop her perpetual motion. She stared, frozen, her breathing quick and shallow.

"Take a deep breath, Amanda. In and out, nice and slow. You're okay."

She did as he asked, closing her eyes and breathing deeply and evenly. Her body trembled under his fingers. *Damn it.* This was his fault.

"Amanda, I didn't mean to upset you. I don't ever want to do anything that scares you."

She sucked in a deep, ragged breath, looking so terribly lost and sad. Her eyelids fluttered open. She stared straight ahead, talking to his chest.

"You don't understand, Blake. There are days when... when everything scares me." Her voice was barely above a whisper. His heart jumped. He thought of that first day, when she ended up unconscious in his arms.

Everything scares me.

She'd kicked her shoes off earlier, and in her bare feet

the top of her head barely reached his shoulders. He put his fingers under her chin and gently tipped her head back.

He wanted to kiss this woman.

Wait. *What?*

No. That would be crazy. He couldn't kiss her. Shouldn't. But how could he not?

Her hair tumbled off her shoulders and down her back in golden curls. Before he knew it, his free hand was slowly twisting into those curls. She didn't pull away. Didn't look away. He lowered his head until his face was just above hers. He felt her breath on his skin. She smelled like citrus and spice and blueberries and red wine. Her lips parted and she stared at him with her enormous eyes.

"I swear I don't want to scare you, Amanda. But…may I kiss you?" His voice was a raw whisper. "Please let me kiss you."

His words came out as a plea. He'd never begged for anything before in his life. But here he was, begging this sweet thing for a kiss. Ready to drop to his knees if that's what it took. He heard his father's voice in his head, mocking his weakness. That's when he started to straighten, coming to his senses. Then he heard her whispered answer.

"Yes."

Was there any sweeter word in the world? Adrenaline surged through his body, and his hand tightened in her hair. His eyes opened to meet those two oceans of blue. Dangerous blue. Deep enough to drown in.

She was frightened, but she was trusting him. And that realization scared *him* to death. He raised his hand to cradle the back of her head as his lips brushed back and forth against hers. She shuddered in his arms and his mouth pressed to hers.

She stiffened for a heartbeat as his tongue ran along her lips. He slid one hand down her back and pulled her into him. He groaned, trying to be careful with her. But he wanted this so bad. A soft sound rose from her throat and, wonder of wonders, she opened her mouth to him. He was almost afraid to go further, but his body had a mind of its own. He tried to hold back, to take it easy, but there was just no damned way to do that. Her hands fluttered nervously at her sides, then moved up to clutch his shoulders. And her tongue...her tongue was pushing into his mouth now. He growled and pulled her closer. He didn't want to let her go. Ever.

When she finally pulled back, she looked up at him in amazement. *Right there with you, sweetheart.* Her knees wobbled, and he wrapped his arm around her lower back to support her.

He dropped his mouth to hers again and she moaned. Her hands slid from his shoulders to the back of his head; her fingers tightened in his hair. She stood on her tiptoes to press up against him. With a jolt, Blake knew he had to stop this before they went too far. Before she pulled him over the edge of the abyss. Just one more swipe around her marvelous mouth...

He set her back and raised his head, trying to gather his bearings. He held her upper arms until she steadied on her feet. They stared at each other in stunned silence.

She lifted her trembling fingers to her lips, which were beautifully swollen now. He could see the struggle in her eyes. The uncertainty. Then she raised those fingers to the side of his face, holding the palm of her hand there against his cheek. He leaned into it. The atmosphere changed in a heartbeat from electric to serene. It was the most intimate moment he could recall in his life.

"I—I—I should go..." She was whispering, stammering. She pulled away and he watched in silence as she left the kitchen. He rested his hands on the edge of the counter and dropped his head, trying to regroup, listening to her footsteps climbing the stairs.

This was bad. And not just because she worked for him. She was vulnerable, and Blake was beginning to realize that he was, as well. He suspected neither of them could handle one more failure, one more heartbreak.

He wouldn't be able to help Amanda any more than he'd been able to help his sister, and he'd adored Tiffany. Losing her had shattered him. That's when he'd built that sturdy wall around his heart. But that carefully constructed wall suffered some major structural damage just now when he'd held Amanda in his arms and kissed her. Something was fluttering and flickering to life inside a heart he thought had broken forever in December.

The earth had just shifted beneath his feet, and he had no idea what the hell was going to happen next.

Chapter Six

Amanda stood on the balcony outside her room and watched the sun come up over the mountains that surrounded Gallant Lake. The untouched mug of coffee in her hand was growing cool. She was still reliving last night. Still reliving that kiss. Trying to figure out what it meant, and what was next.

Intimacy, if a kiss could be considered intimacy, was something she only did reluctantly, because a date expected it. Never because it did anything for her. She thought that part of her—the woman part—had died forever on an October night in Kansas twelve years ago. She'd tried—she wasn't a virgin, for heaven's sake. But those few awkward encounters in college, and some fumbling attempts in recent years, had convinced her she was simply no longer wired to enjoy things like kissing and sex.

But last night… Blake's touch hadn't frightened her. When his lips had touched hers, something inside her had risen up like a phoenix from the ashes of her shattered past. The fire had started in her chest, then spread to every nerve ending in her body. She'd been burning for more. More kisses. More Blake.

And *that's* what frightened her.

She was dressed and ready for the day, but she was standing out here, afraid to face him. She was making herself crazy. She leaned back against the stone wall and sighed. This long, narrow balcony felt like a safe place.

A soft knock on her door made her flinch.

"Amanda? May I come in?" Blake sounded uncharacteristically tentative.

"Yes. I'm outside." She couldn't bring herself to walk in and open the door, and instead listened to his slow footsteps.

He looked away from her as soon as their eyes met. He had regrets. *Damn it.* She looked out over the lake in silence, waiting for him to speak because she couldn't.

"I'm leaving in a few hours." He glanced at her and frowned. "I think I owe you an apol—"

"Don't! Don't you dare apologize." His eyes went wide at the vehemence in her voice. She took a deep breath and continued. "It doesn't ever have to happen again…it shouldn't…it *won't*. But please…don't tell me you're sorry."

He walked to where she stood and stared at her in silence, tilting his head as if trying to read her thoughts.

"I don't regret kissing you, Amanda. I just didn't know how you felt…if I overstepped some boundary." He cleared his throat, put his hands on her shoulders and gave her a boyish grin. "But I am damned sure *not* sorry I kissed you. In fact, I'd very much like to kiss you again."

She put her hand on his chest to keep him from coming closer. Again? Could she stay here if he kissed her again? Would she ever be able to leave?

"Blake, you may do this sort of thing a lot, but I don't. I've never felt what I felt last night, and if it means something different to you, something less than what it was to me, then I can't…"

Her words stopped when his lips touched hers. The kiss was demanding at first, as if he were trying to prove something to her, or to himself. Then he softened his movements and tenderly moved his tongue against hers. He raised his head, then lowered it again and kissed her some more. She couldn't seem to move her body, but her mouth responded, and a low moan rose up from her chest. Her hands finally grabbed on to his shirt and she twisted the fabric beneath her fingers. He growled in return.

He pressed her back against the wall. As soon as her shoulders hit stone, she panicked and started pushing against him. He quickly stepped back and released her.

"I can't…oh, God…" She wrapped her arms tightly across her body, gasping for air. He touched her shoulder, but she shrugged him off. "I'm too much of a mess right now." She gave a short laugh. "Who am I kidding? I've been a hot mess for years. I'm sorry. I'm not capable of doing—"

"Stop." His voice was gentle, and he brushed her cheek with his knuckles. "You're scared. I get it. I pushed too hard. But damn it, Amanda, you make me lose my head." The next words were barely a whisper. "You just make me lose my head."

Her eyes closed at his touch. Her heart was racing. "I still don't understand what any of this means, Blake."

"Neither do I." He took a step back and her skin burned from the loss of his touch. "To be honest, the last thing I want or need is any kind of relationship. I'm no good at them. I don't have the time. But you…" He cleared his throat, and the shutters came down in his eyes. Business Blake was back. "Let's just take it a step at a time, okay? And the next step is me leaving for a while, so we'll both have plenty of time to think it through." He shook his head. "Come have breakfast with me. Oh, and there's a delivery team coming this afternoon with appliances for the kitchen."

She raised an eyebrow at him and he lifted a shoulder in return.

"I'd rather you didn't blow the place up now that I'm spending all this money on it," he teased. "I spoke with Dario last night and he called a restaurant supply friend of his in the city."

Amanda just shook her head. He was back in control of the world around him, which is where he liked to be.

Three hours later, she was standing on the front porch saying goodbye to him.

The delivery team was installing new stainless steel appliances. She stepped aside as three men wheeled in an enormous Sub-Zero refrigerator.

"Hey," Blake said, "I have to go." She looked up at him. Her palms started to sweat. As many times as she'd panicked over a man touching her, she'd *never* felt this burst of fear over one walking away. "I'm not sure how long I'll be gone, but probably close to a month. There's a conference in Honolulu, and then I have to get the Bali project back up to speed." He looked up at the castle behind her. "This is why I gave up on having a home base before now. I'm never in one place for very long. But it's time to settle somewhere. If you have any issues or questions, don't hesitate to reach out. And please don't forget Jamal."

She'd met with Jamal Brickman, the head of security for Gallant Lake Resort, a few days ago. The former marine had worked to put her mind at ease, explaining all of the security measures and cameras. Jamal told her it was all part of Blake's No Surprises Lifestyle. He wanted his security team to *prevent* bad things from happening, not just respond after the fact.

"If anything or anyone bothers you, you contact him immediately, understand?"

She rolled her eyes. "Yes, Dad…"

There was a glimmer of amusement in his eyes. "Never mind your smart mouth." His eyes dropped to her lips. For one brief moment, she thought he was going to kiss her again, and she wanted him to. He raised his hand and gently ran his fingers across her cheek instead.

"I've never hated to leave home before. But here I am, standing like an idiot, just staring at you."

Did he like what he felt, or was he appalled by it? She finally just smiled up at him, saying what needed to be said.

"You'll miss your flight if you don't get going. I'll be fine here. Halcyon likes me." She looked fondly up at the rose-colored tower next to the entrance. "And you're going to like Halcyon when I'm done with it. But you already told me you don't like chaos, and that's all there's going to be for a few weeks. Wait until they start sanding the walls. The place will be an absolute mess."

"It's not the chaos in the house I'm worried about. It's what's going on in your head." He tapped her forehead playfully with his knuckles. "Don't work yourself into knots over this...whatever it is...that's going on with us. Maybe it won't be there when I get back. If it is, we'll figure it out then. But in the meantime, no regrets and no overthinking. We both have jobs to do. Right?"

"Right. Have a safe trip, Blake. I'll keep you posted on the progress."

"Oh, I almost forgot," he said, reaching into his pocket. "Here's the key to the Cadillac. And the remote for the garage." They both looked up the hill to the carriage house.

"Don't worry, I won't put a scratch on your fancy car. Now go, or you really will miss your flight."

They looked at each other silently, then he turned and walked to the waiting limousine without glancing back. She watched the car move around the circular drive and down the hill. It was just her and Halcyon now.

Chapter Seven

A little over a week later, she was seriously questioning her relationship with the old house. She stood in the center of the main hall and sighed. She was hot, dirty and exhausted. The house was a complete disaster zone. They were at that most miserable stage of a renovation, where you had to make things look horrible before you could start making them beautiful. Halcyon had officially reached the apex of horrible.

Dust covered every surface. Strips of stubborn wallpaper still hung from some of the walls, while other walls were paper-free and sanded, ready for paint. But the crew couldn't start painting until *all* the sanding was done. The mingling of all the chemicals and dust had given her a permanent headache. The volume of work still to be done made that headache worse. The huge iron chandeliers were down. Bobby had a friend with a body shop who was going to paint them with a high-gloss auto paint.

In a moment of insanity last week, she'd decided to surprise Blake by redecorating the master suite while he was gone, so the upstairs was a mess, too. Bobby's crew of workers were friendly enough, but it was stressful for her to have a crowd of men she didn't really know in the house day after day. Bobby made sure no one bothered her, but she'd still had a few flutters of panic in the beginning. She'd managed to hide it well. She lifted her camera and started taking more pictures. She couldn't let her panic attacks derail this job. Exhausting as it was, this project would be the foundation of her portfolio so she could start her own design firm, and she needed to document every messy step of the process.

She and Blake had spoken a few times, and texted almost daily, but he seemed to be firmly in business mode while on his trip. He said his days were filled with meetings. Their conversations had been about the house and decisions that had to be made. And that was okay. It proved the kiss they'd shared was an aberration, and it was better for both of them if they just moved on.

"Happy Monday!" Bobby's cheerful voice echoed in the main hall as he came in with five of his men.

"Hi, Bobby. Ready for another week of destruction and mayhem?"

He laughed. "We only have a few more days of stripping and sanding down here, then we'll start painting. Are you ready to have those chandeliers painted? My buddy can pick them up today."

"Yep. Paprika it is. I want the highest gloss possible. It will bring just the right touch of fun to the hall."

Bobby shook his head and smiled. "I still can't picture Mr. Randall liking orange chandeliers, but you're the boss." His workers started filtering in and getting to work. The marble floors were scheduled to be polished next week, so they were going to have to remove all the scaffolding before then. With a little luck, they'd make Blake's Christmas deadline. Bobby looked over her shoulder to the door.

"Hey, little dude. You lost?"

Amanda spun around. A young boy stood in the doorway. Shaggy black hair hung over his chocolate-colored eyes. He looked both defiant and frightened.

"Is my uncle here?" he asked.

Amanda's mouth dropped open. Was this Blake's nephew? The one sent to boarding school?

"Are you Zachary?" The boy nodded cautiously. She stepped toward him. "Hi, my name is Amanda, and I work for your uncle Blake. He's not here. Did he know you were coming?"

Zachary shook his head. "No." He squared his shoulders, his eyes narrowing as if bracing for a confrontation.

She glanced at Bobby, who looked even more baffled than she was. The workers were watching with interest. She could see Blake in the boy's wide brown eyes, and smiled.

"Hi, Zachary. Your uncle told me about you. You're ten, right?" He barely nodded. "Why don't you come in and tell me how you got here."

He stared at her. "Call me Zach. I rode a bus."

Her mouth dropped open. "You took a bus *alone*? Zach, that was so dangerous!"

Zach shrugged. "I know. But I got here."

She was stuck somewhere between shock and laughter. Not only did he have Blake's looks, he had Blake's attitude, too. She stepped aside and he walked into the hall, looking at the renovation with interest.

"Zach, you were lucky. *So* lucky. But yes, you're here. Now tell me why."

"I didn't want to be in school anymore. They were mean to me. So I ran away." His feet shifted. "I won't go back there." His voice got stronger. "I *won't*..."

"Zach," Amanda said, raising her hands to stop him. He watched her carefully. She hoped he could see how sincere she was. "You don't have to go back. Not right now." His small shoulders relaxed. "Have you been to Halcyon before?"

He nodded. "Once. Last winter. After my mom died. Didn't look like this, though."

This poor child had been through a lot. "I'm sorry about your mom, Zach. I'm going to call your uncle and let him know you're here, okay? Are you hungry?"

He hesitated, and Bobby stepped forward. "I'll take him down to the resort for something to eat while you call

Mr. Randall." He smiled at Zach. "My name's Bobby, and I'm a friend of Miss Amanda's. Let's go grab some food, then you can help us work on this old place, okay?"

Zach gave Bobby that calm, much-older-than-ten gaze, then slowly followed Bobby out the door.

Amanda reached for her phone, glancing at her watch. It was eleven o'clock. In Hawaii it was, what...five in the morning? He was probably asleep, but he needed to know. She sent a quick text.

Zachary is at Halcyon.

Her phone rang almost immediately. She hadn't heard his voice in a while, and she'd never heard him this furious.

"What the hell? He's supposed to be at Beakman Academy. What happened?"

"Zach ran away. He said they were mean to him."

Blake gave a heavy sigh. "Yeah, well, Zach inherited his mother's flair for drama. How the hell did he get there?"

"Believe it or not, he took a bus."

"Excuse me?"

"He took a bus. Alone."

"A *bus*. From Connecticut."

"When I pointed out how dangerous it was, he basically said, 'I got here, didn't I?'"

Blake barked out a laugh.

"I know it's not funny, but damn, that kid's gonna kill me yet. Let me talk to him."

"He's down at the resort with Bobby. I figured he was hungry."

He paused. "Right. Okay, I'll call Beakman and see what happened. In the meantime, I'll see if my sister-in-law will come get him."

Amanda didn't hesitate. "He can stay here. I'll watch him."

There was something about the kid—maybe the loneliness in his eyes, or the defiance—that touched her heart.

Blake sounded stunned. "You? You're running a major renovation project. Now you want to be my nephew's nanny, too?" She was being impulsive, which wasn't her usual style. But she felt strongly that Zach belonged here. Blake blew out a long breath. "You've seriously blown my mind with this call. Zach's there now, so…sure, if you don't mind, keep him with you for a couple days. I'll call the academy to smooth things over."

"I'm happy to take care of him. But please reconsider the academy, Blake. Something happened there. And he's so young."

"He's had a rough year, Amanda. The school gives him the structure he needs."

"But—"

"This is a family matter, and I'll handle it. Just watch him for a couple of days until I can make some calls. Okay?"

"Fine."

"Thank you. I'll be in touch."

And he was gone. She was now responsible for the safety and well-being of a ten-year-old boy she'd just met.

Life here at Gallant Lake just kept getting more and more interesting.

Chapter Eight

Zach lay down on the old chaise in the living room after he and Bobby returned and fell fast asleep, even with all the work going on around him. When he finally woke, he joined Bobby in sanding the walls. He was reserved, but by the time the workers left, he'd started to relax. He must have started to trust Amanda's promise that he really was going to stay at Halcyon. At least for now.

They talked a little over dinner, and he told her how some of the boys in his class had started bullying him, hassling him about having a mom who was a "druggie." It went from verbal to physical, and *Zach* was the one who got in trouble when he'd fought back. When it had happened again, he'd decided to leave.

"My mom told me it was wrong to get mad and fight. She said people should get along. But..." He took another big bite of the brownies she'd baked. "That didn't work. Uncle Blake said he was here if I needed him, and I figured I did. I knew there was a bus that came this way, and the old lady at the station helped me. I told her my grandma was sick. She had me sit with her until the bus came, then she yelled at the driver to let me sit behind him."

Amanda closed her eyes, sending a silent prayer of thanks that a kindhearted stranger made sure Zach stayed safe on his foolhardy journey. She could see he was still tired, so they went upstairs shortly after dinner. She checked the dresser in his room, relieved to find a few clothes that looked like they'd still fit him. Zach's face fell when he looked at the bed, covered with teddy bears.

She smiled. "I bet Bobby and I can make this room look a little more grown-up for you. Maybe paint it in the color of a sports team you like?"

His face brightened. "Can we do pinstripes? For my favorite baseball team?"

"I'm sure we can come up with something like that." The suite was the mirror image of Blake's, with a circular sitting area and fireplace. She looked at the door that opened to the small balcony. A third-floor balcony was a bad idea for a child's room. She walked over and tried to turn the knob, but the door didn't even jiggle, as if it was sealed shut.

Thanks, Madeleine.

She didn't *actually* believe in ghosts, but she'd started blaming, or thanking, the legendary ghost of Halcyon for anything she couldn't explain in the house—from strange noises at night to curtains that seemed to move without a breeze. Old houses were full of mysteries like that. Like sealed balcony doors.

"Are you and Uncle Blake going to get married?"

Amanda started coughing violently, caught off guard by Zach's unexpected question.

"No! No." She caught her breath. "No, Zach. We're… friends. I work for your uncle."

"But you live here."

"That's only temporary, while I oversee the remodeling." The idea of leaving Gallant Lake made her sad. The fact that she had no idea where she'd live or what she'd do made her anxious. But at least she had some company while she was here—it had been lonely since Blake had left. She grinned at Zach.

"And now *you* live here, too. Temporarily, at least."

Zach jumped to his feet. "I won't go back to Beakman! If you try to make me go, I'll run away again."

"*Why*, Zach?"

"I hate it there." He dropped his head. "Last week was

parents' weekend, and no one came. That's when the other boys started teasing me."

"Oh, Zach, I'm so sorry. Your uncle was in Hawaii, so he couldn't possibly..." It only took one accusing glare from the boy to silence her defense of Blake. Because leaving this kid on his own at a boarding school was indefensible. What was *wrong* with Blake and his family? Why weren't they taking better care of Zach?

"Let's take things one day at a time, okay, Zach? For now, you're here with me, and you can help Bobby and me with the house until we figure out the school situation. Maybe you can go to school in Gallant Lake..." She never should have said that aloud, but Zach jumped on it.

"You mean *stay* here? For real? Could I ride the school bus? I've never ridden a school bus! Would I be here for Christmas?"

She pulled some pajamas from the dresser. "That's up to your uncle." She tossed the pajamas on the bed and gestured toward it. "It's time for bed. And, Zach?"

He looked at her with cautious brown eyes. "Yeah?"

"I promise I'll talk to your uncle about school, but I want *you* to promise you won't run away from here. From me. You're going to have to trust me, okay? And *stay*?"

It was either that or she'd have to sleep outside his door every night to make sure he stayed put. But he nodded.

"I promise. But I'm *not* going back."

He was asleep within minutes. Amanda sent a text message to Blake from her room.

Please don't send him back to Beakman.

Blake didn't respond, so she waited. A full day passed, and no reply. She texted again.

We need to talk. Zach can't go to Beakman.

Nothing.

After a few days of awkward and often one-sided conversations between Zach and her, Zach seemed to have decided that Amanda was not only *okay*, but was also his guardian angel. Probably because she hadn't sent him away. He'd hugged her for the first time the day after his arrival. Once she'd recovered from her surprise, she'd hugged him back.

He seemed to crave human contact. She wasn't normally a hugger, but she made an exception for Zach. Especially after he told her one night that his mom used to hug him all the time. If he needed her to be a surrogate mom, that was okay with her. For one thing, it meant he was less likely to try to run away. And for another…she found *she* was getting as much from those hugs as he was.

They established their ground rules quickly. He had to be sure she always knew where he was. If he went down to the resort, he had to obey Miss Julie and Mr. Jamal. Zach followed Bobby around Halcyon all day, so Bobby put him to work pulling off wallpaper and sanding walls.

His uncle seemed to have just forgotten about him, but Zach should be in school somewhere. It felt as if no one in the Randall family wanted to give any thought to this lonely little boy. She wondered how his mother died, but she didn't want to ask him to talk about it. Her own father had died at Christmastime when she was young. Was he seeing a counselor? Did anyone think to get help for him? Her fretfulness over Zach's well-being shook her to the core. She wanted to look after him the way that no one had when she was young.

When Blake ignored her third text in three days *and* a voice mail, she angrily decided to take matters into her own hands. She cared about Zach, even if no one else did. She talked to Julie, who had friends at the local elementary school. Amanda took Zach to the school and they met Bruce

Hoffman, a fourth-grade teacher. The principal, Elizabeth Cantore, sat in on the meeting. Zach liked Mr. Hoffman, and Amanda did, too. The teacher's dark hair was pulled back into a low ponytail. Dressed in chinos and a chambray shirt with Birkenstocks on his bare feet, his eyes were kind and he seemed genuine. An hour later, it was all arranged.

Zach would attend school as Zachary Lowery to protect his identity. The Randall name was well-known in Gallant Lake, and not in a good way. Even Bruce admitted taking part in protests against the casino, but he vowed he'd never saddle Zach with that. Zach was more excited about riding the school bus than anything else.

She finally heard from Blake that evening. She was just settling into bed when her phone chirped with a text message.

I talked to the headmaster at Beakman. They've agreed to give him another chance. They'll send a car for him.

Her response was almost as swift as the rush of anger she felt.

That's a bad decision. Really bad. The worst.

Her phone rang in her hand. Blake. Finally. He didn't wait for her greeting, just started right in. "Not that it's any of your business, but why is it a bad decision?"

"Well, for one thing, you haven't even asked *why* he ran away. They bullied him, Blake. And when he reported it to the headmaster, they didn't believe him. That's why I've been trying to reach you. He can't go back there. Please..." Her emotions overwhelmed her, and her voice broke. Blake was quiet for a moment, and was much calmer when he spoke again.

"I didn't know that."

"Of course not, because you never returned my messages. Do you know *why* it got so bad? Because none of your family went to the parents' weekend. He was the only one with no family there, Blake, and the kids picked on him."

"Shit. I meant to ask Nathan to go." He sighed. "I can never seem to do the right thing for him. I don't know *how* to do the right thing. I have no idea why Tiffany left him to *me* of all people…"

She couldn't argue that he was making a mess of being Zach's guardian, but she also felt a stab of pity for him. He sounded lost. "It's okay, Blake. He's fine now, and he likes it here in Gallant Lake. I've enrolled him in the local school…"

"Public school is not the answer, Amanda. A good private school will give Zach what he needs. I'll talk to Beakman and make sure they keep an eye on things, but Randalls don't go to public schools—"

"But he wants to go to school here, and he's really excited about it. Please, Blake…"

"Of course he *wants* to. But you can't just let children do whatever they want. He doesn't get to make this type of decision for himself. The answer is no." His voice was firm and businesslike. "I'm headed to Bali tomorrow, so communication will be sketchy, but I'll have Beakman contact you to let you know when they'll pick him up. He'll be fine. Tell him he can come back to Halcyon for Christmas."

"But, Blake…"

"Amanda, I have a meeting to get to. I'm sorry you got caught up in this family mess, and I really am grateful for what you've done for the boy. I'll pay you for your time and trouble. I know he can be difficult."

"This isn't about money!" She didn't give a damn about his money. "He is *not* difficult! He's a kind, loving little boy. He needs a stable home that makes him feel safe. He loves it here at Halcyon. He wants to ride the bus to school with the kids in Gallant Lake…"

"That is not going to happen. He'll be fine. I'll be in touch." And he was gone.

She leaned back against the headboard of her bed. What Blake didn't know wouldn't hurt him, right? She was going to send Zach to school tomorrow in Gallant Lake as planned, and she'd deal with the Beakman situation somehow. She'd fibbed to get this job, so what was one more little lie? She wasn't going to let Zach sit home while Blake wasted his time messing about.

A week later, her cousin's silence on the other end of the phone call spoke volumes.

"Say *something*, Nora." Amanda stared out at the blue waters of the lake from her balcony. It was early October and days were turning cooler, but today the sun was shining bright and warm. Her cousin's unexpected call seemed like a sign from the universe that she needed to tell *someone* about the mess she'd gotten herself into. Zach had been going to the local school, and he loved it. But it wouldn't be long before Blake learned she'd told the headmaster at Beakman Academy that plans had changed and they no longer needed to send a car for Zachary. And once Blake knew, everything was going to come crashing down. She was trapped between doing what was right for Zach and being fair to Blake.

"Nora?"

"I don't even know where to start, Mandy. You kissed this guy, and you actually *liked* it, then he left, you tore his house apart, and now you're taking care of his nephew? Alone? The school let you enroll him without being his guardian?"

"I talked really fast, and Julie may have suggested to the principal that I was his legal guardian before I even got there." Julie was the only other person who knew she'd lied to allow Zach to stay. Everyone else thought it was Blake's idea.

"You're turning into quite the little grifter, honey. I should be appalled, but I'm honestly impressed." Amanda wasn't sure how she felt about this new dishonest side of herself, either. Nora's Southern accent deepened as her worry did. "But, honey, what happens when Blake finds out? Mel said he's pretty intense. Doesn't sound like the type to be amused by any of this. You're getting attached to this boy, and he could be snatched away from you in the blink of an eye. Are you ready for that? Is Zach? Did you really think this through?" Every word hit home for Amanda because she asked herself the very same questions every night.

"Clearly not. But I'm in it now. Blake doesn't see Zach as anything but a burden right now. Maybe when he gets back… I don't know." She shook her head and leaned back against the wall of Halcyon, which felt oddly warm on this chilly evening. "The kid is just so lost and lonely." Amanda closed her eyes and rubbed the bridge of her nose. "I know this could end up being an absolute disaster for everyone. I just have to hope that it's not."

"Have you been talking to Dr. Jackson?"

Amanda blinked a few times in surprise. "Once. We had a phone session a few weeks ago."

Dr. Jackson had been supportive of Amanda taking on the design project at Halcyon, and was thrilled to hear she and Blake had shared a few kisses with no panic attacks. The doctor had been encouraging her for months be more spontaneous, and she, like Nora, thought Gallant Lake was inspiring Amanda's impulsive side. But Dr. Jackson knew nothing about Zach's arrival. She may have taken the idea of being spontaneous a little too far.

Nora broke the silence. "You're taking a lot of chances, and I worry about all the things that could go wrong. You were already having panic attacks…" Her voice drifted off.

Tension simmered under Amanda's skin. Yes, exhaustion was catching up to her. Worrying about Zach, and Blake's reaction to what she'd done, along with the construction chaos and worrying the protestors might show up at the entrance to Halcyon and hassle Zach—it was all wearing on her.

"I'm okay." She had to say it, even if she didn't believe it. "Really, I am. I appreciate you calling me, Nora." She stood shakily and brushed away the tears she didn't realize she'd started to shed. "I have to go. Zach will be home any minute, and he likes it when I meet the bus. Keep me in your prayers, coz."

"Every day, girl. Every day."

She did her best to put up a brave front for Zach, but the strain wore at her as the days passed. Two nights later, he found her sitting on the floor in the solarium, weeping uncontrollably. He'd curled up at her side, hugged her tight and told her not to cry. Which, of course, made her cry more.

And nightmares…well, the nightmares were back with a vengeance. The workers were making her edgy, and Bobby had to fire one that week for wearing a T-shirt with a vulgarity on it referring to the casino plans. Bobby told the guy to go change and the man started yelling about "free speech" and how Blake Randall was "killing Gallant Lake." Bobby fired him on the spot. Did the other workers feel the same hatred for Blake and the resort? The confrontation sent her spiraling into a persistent state of anxiety. Her nerves were frayed. Every passing day added to the amount of trouble she'd be in when Blake discovered Zach was still at Halcyon.

Maybe it was selfish, but she needed Zach as much as he needed her. Halcyon was different since he'd arrived. Warmer. Brighter. So she pushed herself through each day with a smile and tried to ignore the firestorm that was surely headed her way.

Chapter Nine

Blake shook with anger as he marched through the airport in Sydney, Australia. Ten days ago, he'd called Amanda about sending Zach to Beakman. Ten *freakin'* days.

She'd begged him to put the boy in public school, but that was a nonstarter. He slowed his pace a bit as he headed for his gate. His sister, of course, would have loved the idea of her little boy being the first Randall to break the private school tradition. But as much as he'd adored Tiffany, she'd thrown her life away, and now it was up to Blake to make sure Zachary had a proper upbringing.

Amanda finally assured him that she would have Zach ready to go when Beakman sent someone. He'd checked his nephew off on his mental to-do list days ago and focused on getting construction on the new resort back up to speed. The Blake Randall No Surprises Lifestyle was firmly back in place. Until yesterday.

Yesterday was when he got a call from the headmaster, wondering where to send Zach's things, since he wasn't returning. Blake thought he was going to burst a blood vessel right there on the spot.

There wasn't a doubt in his mind that Zachary was riding a school bus to the tired little school in Gallant Lake, getting who knows what for an education. And Amanda *lied* about it. She lied to *him*. About his *family*. He gave the headmaster some excuse about a "miscommunication" and booked his flight home.

The outright gall of the woman, to openly defy him over a family issue that had nothing to do with her! Apparently he'd badly misjudged her common sense. She had to know she'd be finished as soon as he discovered what she'd done.

He walked down the gangway to the plane and frowned. He should have known about Zach before now, of course. He should have checked on his nephew. It rankled him that he wouldn't have known anything was amiss if the school hadn't called him. He would have shown up in Gallant Lake in a week or two and...what?

He fell into his first-class seat with a sigh and shook his head. That woman had big brass ones, all right. She probably figured she was safe because he hadn't communicated with her much while he was traveling. That silence had been very intentional. Every time he heard Amanda's sweet voice, his longing for her increased. He needed his focus, and she messed with that just by breathing a few words into the phone from thousands of miles away.

It started when she sent him that picture a few weeks ago of herself on the ladder in her tight jeans and ball cap, ponytail dangling down her back, laughing at the camera. When he saw the photo on his phone, it took every ounce of strength not to leave the meeting he was in and jump on the next flight to be with her. The woman was bad for business. She was bad for him.

She knew he was going to find out about Zach eventually. She was probably sweating bullets over it right now. What kind of crazy plan did she have? He shook his head grimly and pulled out his phone. It was time to make her squirm. He tapped out a text.

How's the house coming? Any problems getting Zach to go back to school?

He waited so long he thought he was going to have to turn off the phone before she answered. The jet's doors were just closing when his phone finally chirped.

House is great. Furniture arriving. Zach loves school.

He laughed out loud, ignoring the looks from his fellow passengers. She didn't quite lie, did she? She didn't say *which* school. Did she think she could get away with dancing that fine line for long? He'd be in Gallant Lake tomorrow, and he couldn't wait to see her face when he arrived. He sent her a quick reply just as the flight attendant asked him to shut off the phone.

Glad to hear it. See you in a couple weeks.

It was a long twenty-four-hour journey with very little sleep, and he was simmering with angry anticipation when he finally arrived at JFK. Amanda had single-handedly blown his No Surprises plan right out of the water. He had the evidence to throw in her face, which was exactly what he'd do when he saw her.

He leaned back against the seat. Why didn't he feel better about it?

Amanda paced the main hall at Halcyon restlessly. The house was empty and quiet. Bobby's crew was off today, working on a charity home-build down in White Plains. Zach was in school. She walked into the living room and looked at the freshly painted walls. She frowned when she saw a few uneven spots near the ceiling, above the doorway. She sighed. It was going to bother her until she fixed it.

The painting crew's twelve-foot stepladder was nearby, along with paint and an assortment of brushes. She glanced down at her clothes. These old jeans and sweatshirt were perfect for painting. The job would help keep her mind off Blake.

She was standing on the ladder with her back to it, leaning forward to reach a spot above the doorway to the main hall. Humming to herself, she gently smoothed the uneven lines with a small angled brush. She never heard the limo pull up in front of the big house. Didn't hear footsteps cross the stone porch. But she certainly heard the front door fly open with a crash. The sound nearly upended her, and she leaned back against the shaking ladder to steady herself.

"Amanda!"

How on earth could Blake be *here*? He'd just sent a text from Bali yesterday. Her heart dropped. The day she'd been dreading had arrived earlier than expected. He knew Zach wasn't at boarding school. And he'd flown halfway around the world to confront her in person. He shouted her name up the staircase.

His jaw was set, his brows drawn together, and his body was tight and tense. Dressed for the islands in linen slacks and a white cotton shirt, he looked even more handsome than she remembered. When he spun in her direction and spotted her up on the ladder, his eyes were blazing. There was a flicker of surprise, perhaps even concern, as he registered that she was at least ten feet above the floor. Her palms started to sweat.

"What are you doing up there?" He started marching in her direction.

"Um…painting…" Her voice sounded like a squeak in her own ears. *Steady, girl, steady.*

"The idea was not for you to actually *do* the work, Amanda. Come down before you fall."

He had a right to be angry. She'd caused this mess. She studied his stony face, then shook her head. "I think I'll stay right here."

She moved another step up on the ladder, so her bottom was sitting on the very top. The ladder shuddered, and she reached down to grab either side of her seat. His hands shot out to steady the ladder from below.

"For God's sake, Amanda, I have no intention of snatching you off this thing."

The gleaming marble floor was a long way down. It was bad enough that Blake was about to break her heart. Falling off this ladder wasn't going to help matters. She carefully slid down so that she was sitting on the second step from the top. Once she was settled, she raised one brow and gave him her most calm and collected expression. She knew she was about to be fired. Might as well go out with attitude, right?

"So...you wanted to talk?"

If the moment wasn't so serious, she would have laughed out loud at the way he sputtered at her bravado. Then he slowly shook his head and leveled a glare at her. Now that he was no longer worried, he'd found his anger again.

"Do you have any idea how stupid I felt when the headmaster called to ask where to send Zach's things? How furious I was when I realized you must have enrolled him in a *public* school after I told you not to?" He ran an agitated hand through his hair as she watched, wide-eyed and silent. His voice rose to a bellow, echoing off the walls. "Just who the *hell* do you think you are, Amanda Lowery? You're not Zach's guardian. You're not even his family! You're just an employee who can't follow simple instructions."

She stiffened. "Just an employee, huh? Well, that doesn't say much for your parenting skills, does it? Because when your nephew needed you, you pawned him off on this 'employee' you barely know." She struck her chest with her hand. She thought about her own childhood, when her stepfather ignored her at her darkest hour. "You just kept working on your big important hotel projects halfway around the world. You didn't even call to see how he was doing. It took you all this time to realize he wasn't at Beakman. As long as you could stay uninvolved in his problems and send him away again, you were happy as a clam, weren't you?"

He took a step backward, looking stunned by her fierce words. She was just getting started.

"He's a little boy, Blake! A little boy with no parents, and a family who clearly views him as some annoying burden. Do you think he doesn't see how unimportant he is to all of you?"

"He's *not* unimportant. I'm spending a hell of a lot of money on his education…"

She threw her hands up. The motion made the ladder shake, and Blake reached out to grab it again as she spat her words down at him.

"Money! That's all you care about!"

She gestured wildly, and Blake cursed as he held the ladder.

"Come down here, goddamn it, before you fall."

She ignored him. She'd been nursing her rage for days now, and she wasn't about to hold back. Not anymore.

"I don't know what's going on with your family, Blake, but you are all seriously screwed up. This child—and he is a *child*—lost his mother, and is unwanted by anyone in his own family. You farm him out to private schools when he's only *ten years old*. My God, he's a scared, lonely little boy who just wants to have a childhood. What is wrong with you people?"

Blake's eyes narrowed again, and a muscle twitched in his cheek. He was pissed off. Well, good. So was she. His voice was raw with emotion when he finally responded.

"How *dare* you suggest that I don't care about Zachary! He's my sister's son. I don't want Zach to be weak like his mother was. He needs discipline and structure. Beakman is not a prison. It's a school, where he'll be safe and will have someone directing him…"

She shook her head sadly, tears burning at her eyes. She wasn't sure who she felt sorrier for—Zach or Blake. "He's not weak. He's terrified. He's lonely. He doesn't need direction. He needs *love*," Blake rolled his eyes and groaned.

"Oh, yeah, that's right. Love solves everything. Let me know how that works out for you in that Pollyanna world you seem to be living in. Because here in the real world, it's hard work and education that pave the way to success. Love is a ridiculous, frivolous emotion. My sister was chasing love when she died. My mother was chasing love when she abandoned her children. And aren't you chasing it right now by pretending to be Zach's mother?"

His words hit her heart like a box cutter blade— sharp, straight and deep. Blake pointed at her, not done yet.

"Love is like fool's gold, Amanda. Love is an illusion. A trick. A flicker of a moment that's not worth the resulting trouble."

She stared at Blake's hard face, trying to process his words. Did he really believe that? What hope was there for Zachary if he did? What hope was there for her? Deflated, she started moving slowly down the ladder. She stopped on that last step and looked at him sadly.

"Zach is a little boy who is full of love. And he has no one to give it to. How exactly is that going to work out for *him*, Blake?"

He blinked and looked away from her. His voice sounded hollow. "Little boys grow up. He just has to do it a little sooner than most. He'll survive. I did."

"At what cost?"

She whispered the words, but he flinched as if she'd slapped him. Before he could speak, she stepped off the ladder and moved to brush past him. Her heart was a cold, leaden weight in her chest. "I may just be an employee who disobeyed orders. But your nephew is happy at the Gallant Lake school. He's making friends. He does his homework every night. He's a really good kid, Blake. He deserves more than what you had."

He put his hand on her arm and spun her around. She had no choice but to meet his angry stare. "More? *More?* You don't know what you're talking about. I had everything. I was raised in a life of privilege, just like Zach will be. He'll make his mark in the world, just as every generation of Randalls has done. That's what's expected…" His voice trailed off as if he suddenly doubted his own words. As if he were reciting a family mantra that had been forcefed to him.

Her anger flared afresh. "And how has that worked out for *you*, Blake? You were given 'everything'…" She raised her fingers to make air quotes. "How much 'everything' do you need to be satisfied? Is this house enough?" She gestured to the grand staircase. "Or maybe you should defy the courts and tear this down along with all the other properties to build your big casino. Will that be enough? Will ruining an entire community be enough for you?" Her voice hardened even as her tears spilled over. She was ending whatever hope they had for a future. Those wonderful kisses were nothing more than a bittersweet memory. "And what will be enough for Zach? Will he have to be richer than you to have 'everything'? Own more properties? Have more success? Isn't that what already broke his mother?"

His hand tightened on her arm.

"Don't you talk about his mother! Don't you *dare* talk about Tiffany like you knew her. You didn't know her at all. You don't know me. You don't know a damned thing, Amanda. Do you hear me?"

His voice rose with every sentence until he was shouting. She blanched in the face of his fury. His grip wasn't painful, but she felt panic rising in her chest. Or was it heartbreak? Tears poured down her face and she raised her hands to push him away. He was too close. It was too much.

"Let her go!"

Zachary stood in the doorway. Her heart dropped. How

much had he heard? Zach ran in from the main hall and launched himself at Blake's back, pummeling his uncle's broad shoulders with small fists.

"Let her go, Uncle Blake! Don't you hurt her! Let her go!"

Chapter Ten

Blake had no choice but to release Amanda so he could deflect Zach's blows. He turned to focus on his nephew, catching Zach's arms gently in his hands and dropping to his knees.

"Zachary, stop!" Blake's voice was firm but calm. "I would never hurt her..." Over Zach's shoulder, he saw Amanda run up the stairs. He felt a searing flash of guilt. He'd put his hands on her in anger. The thought made him sick.

"I saw you! She's the only person who's been nice to me and you made her cry! She cries so much..." Zach's brown eyes were wide and overflowing with tears. Appalled, Blake pulled the little boy into his arms.

Wait. What had he said? Blake held Zach out at arm's length again.

"What do you mean 'she cries so much'? Why does Amanda cry, Zach?"

Zach shrugged, sniffling at his tears. Blake handed him a handkerchief and sat back on his heels while Zach blew his nose and dried his eyes.

"She was crying in the sunny room last week. And she has nightmares..."

"Nightmares?"

Zach nodded solemnly. "She screams really loud."

A chill settled over Blake's heart. Nightmares. Alone in this big house. The thought was so disturbing he barely noticed Zach was speaking again.

"She won't let me in there, Uncle Blake. She locked her

door after the first time. She said she's afraid she'll hurt me, but she'd never do that."

Blake dropped his head into his hands and groaned. What the hell had been happening in this house while he was intentionally avoiding them? While he was too far away to know or care that a frightened woman and his lonely nephew were barely holding each other together here without him. The same way he'd left Zach alone with Tiffany while she fought her demons. The kid was only ten years old. Was there any relationship Blake *couldn't* screw up?

"A bad man scared her."

Blake looked up sharply at those words. Staring straight into those brown eyes that reminded him so much of his sister's, Blake forced his voice to sound light and unconcerned. He didn't want to show the panic that Zach's words incited in him.

"Tell me what you mean by that, Zach. What bad man?" He thought of those sleazy guys hanging out with the protestors. Did someone harass her?

"She said it was a long time ago. Sometimes she sees the guy in her sleep and has nightmares."

A long time ago? She got upset when he asked her about her childhood. What the hell had happened to her? His face burned with shame, thinking how he'd just grabbed her like an angry brute.

"Zach, do you know where Amanda went?"

His nephew frowned. "Probably to the balcony in her room. She likes it up there." Zach fixed him with a stern look. "Don't hurt her."

"I won't. I promise." He swallowed hard, hating that his nephew thought him capable of hurting Amanda. "I'm going to apologize for scaring her. Why don't you do your homework while I do that, okay?"

Zach studied him solemnly, then nodded. "Can I use the living room?"

"Of course. And, Zach?" Blake caught Zach's hand as the boy started to turn away. "I want you to know that I would *never* intentionally hurt Amanda. Hurting girls is a very bad thing to do. You know that, right?"

Zach stared back, wide-eyed. He looked so much like his mother, with that intriguing blend of innocence and wisdom.

Blake sighed. "Do you like your school?"

The boy's eyes lit up. "Yeah! Mr. Hoffman is cool, and the kids are nice. And I get to ride the school bus!"

Blake gave the boy a quick, awkward hug. Things hadn't been easy for Zach, and Blake really didn't know what to do for the kid. He winced at the realization that he'd basically done nothing at all. Amanda was right. He just kept sending him away. She was probably the first person to show Zach any true affection since his mother died.

"I'm glad you like it. Now go do your homework. We'll all go down to the resort for dinner in a while." Zach dashed into the living room with his backpack. Blake took the stairs two at a time. Would Amanda forgive him?

Could he forgive himself?

She was sitting on the stone railing of the balcony, her feet dangling on either side of the waist-high wall. Her back was braced against the tower, but it was still a precarious position far above the stone veranda. Blake had never been fond of heights, but apparently Amanda had no such fear, scampering up ladders and sitting on balcony walls.

God, she was beautiful, even more so than he remembered. Her hair was pulled up into a ponytail high on her head, showing off her long neck and pretty face. She'd put everything she had—her only job and her only home—on the line for his nephew. She had bravely gone to work picking up the pieces of the little boy's shattered life.

She quickly wiped tears from her cheeks with the back of her hand when she noticed him there. She raised her chin defiantly, gazing out over Gallant Lake before turning to slide off her perch. Still avoiding his face, she started to push past him.

"I'll start packing my things…"

His arm slipped around her waist to stop her forward motion. They stood like that in silence, side by side, facing opposite directions, with only his arm connecting them. He slowly pulled her closer, and she inhaled sharply when their bodies came in contact. He reached across and cupped her chin in his hand, turning her face toward his. He gazed into her wide eyes, which were glistening with unshed tears. Neither of them appeared to breathe.

"Let me go…" Stress and exhaustion were etched on her face. There were dark shadows under her brilliant eyes. She'd been shouldering far too much in his absence. His chest tightened. He was such an idiot.

"Damn it, Amanda…" The words came out on a breath, soft and ragged. He dropped his head and rested it against hers. "Sit with me so we can talk. I'm sorry, okay? I never meant to frighten you. As angry as I was, I never wanted to do that." He pressed a chaste kiss on her forehead. "And please, no more talk about packing. I don't want you to go."

He released her, and for a terrifying moment he thought she was leaving. But she only walked as far as one of the wicker chairs, where she sat with a sigh. He pulled another chair close and sat facing her, their knees nearly touching. She stared out at the lake.

"Look at me, Amanda."

Her eyelashes swept up and her blue eyes locked on his. Time had done nothing to cool the attraction between them. Those eyes still managed to leave him breathless. He cleared his throat and tried to focus, running his hand through his hair in frustration.

"I'm sorry for what happened downstairs, more than you can know. If I hurt you…or scared you… There's no excuse for putting my hands on you that way, and I swear to God I'll never do it again."

She stared at him as if she was trying to gauge his sincerity. For once in his life, he wanted someone to see his pain. He wanted her to know how much anguish he was feeling over what he'd done.

She finally nodded. "We were both pretty heated, weren't we? I... I know I overstepped my bounds with Zach. I *do* know that..."

"You did. But that doesn't excuse my behavior. Please forgive me, Amanda." Here he was, begging again. They looked at each other in silence.

"I forgive you." His entire body relaxed. Her forgiveness shouldn't mean so much, but it did. Apparently, it meant everything.

Her forehead wrinkled in concern.

"I shouldn't have said what I did about your family. About you and Zach."

"I'm pretty angry about that." He rushed to explain when her face paled. "But only because it's so true. My family *is* totally screwed up, Amanda. I know it. I just don't like hearing it. It's one of those things where I can bitch about them, but no one else can. My family is a train wreck. My mother is a gold-digging shrew. My father is a cold, unemotional son of a bitch. My sister was a drug addict. And my brother is a spineless coward controlled by his wife and his father."

"I didn't tell you the truth about Zach and school."

"No, you didn't." He waited for her to explain.

"I know it wasn't my decision to make. He was so upset, and I couldn't get you to listen to me. I felt like I was the only person protecting Zach." He winced at the truth in her words. She blinked back tears, but a couple escaped and rolled down her cheek. He reached out and wiped them away with his fingertips while she kept talking. "And he's so much happier now,..he loves Gallant Lake..."

"He said he likes the school and his teacher."

Her eyes went wide and a smile danced across those crazy beautiful lips of hers. "He really does love it. He's doing great."

"Randalls aren't exactly popular in this town. Some of the protesters are more aggressive than the others. I don't think anything will happen, but they're...unpredictable." He thought again of those angry younger men mingling with the usual picketers. "There's no protection for him at that school."

"Bruce and the principal are the only ones who know who Zach is."

"Bruce?"

"His teacher. Bruce Hoffman. I enrolled Zach under my last name. Bruce watches out for him and keeps a close eye on him when the kids are outdoors. Bruce also makes sure Zach gets on the bus without a problem."

Blake was torn between appreciation for Amanda's handling of the situation, and a slow-burning rage every time she said the word "Bruce" the way she did. Like they were friends. Like they were close.

"Sounds like you and *Bruce* have spent some time talking about this."

She shrugged. "We had dinner at the resort and I explained the situation to him. He's with Zach all day, and I felt he should know what to watch for, between security and everything Zach's dealing with emotionally..."

"You had dinner..." Blake swallowed an illogical rush of anger and tried to focus on the matter at hand. "I have to say, Amanda, I was afraid you were taking Zach's situation too lightly, but you covered all the bases. Except for telling me what you were doing." He raked his fingers through his hair. "I can't imagine what my family will say about him going to public school, but it's my decision to make."

"He just wants to have a home with you."

He dropped his head and shook it. "I don't know how to raise a boy."

Why the hell had Tiffany trusted *him* with her son? What did she see in him that he didn't see in himself? And here he was screwing it all up.

Amanda looked at him curiously. "How did that happen? How did the single guy end up as Zach's guardian when your brother is married and has children?"

He shrugged. That was the question of the hour, wasn't it? "Tiffany stipulated me as Zachary's guardian in her will. She and I were close as kids. She was only a year younger than me. Mother always said the back-to-back pregnancies ruined her body or something, and blamed Tiffany specifically, since she was unplanned. I always tried to protect her. Clearly, I failed in the end..."

"Blake..." Amanda reached out and put her small hand over his. He huffed out a soft laugh, looking out over the lake.

"You know, I can still see Tiffie as a little girl at our place on Long Island." He could picture her as clearly as if she was right there in front of him. Her long dark hair whipping around her face, running in the sand, challenging the boys to race into the waves. He looked back to Amanda and smiled. "She was an undeniable force of energy. Very artistic—she loved creating things. Her favorite time of year was Christmas. She was always laughing, always plotting some practical joke, always getting into trouble with our father. I tried to deflect Dad's anger from her, but that just made it worse. He'd punish her more harshly for 'lowering' me to her level of irresponsibility. And responsibility is the gold standard in the Randall household. That and *winning*. Tiffany never cared about any of that." He paused, realizing it had been a long time since he'd talked about his sister. "She was the kid who would be leading the race but turn back to help someone who stumbled. She actually did that once, and Dad grounded her for a month for being 'stupid.'"

"Poor Tiffany." Amanda squeezed his hand. All of his childhood memories, even the good ones, inevitably lead to pain.

"Mother left us for some Italian race car driver when Tiff was around seven, and we stayed with Dad. When Tiffany realized she'd never win either parent's love or approval, she turned to a different crowd of friends, and got into drugs. I was away at school. By the time I saw it, it was too late. She was out of control. If she ever knew who Zach's father was, she never admitted it. At least she knew enough to stop that shit while she was pregnant, but by his first birthday she was right back with her old crowd and old ways. The rest of the family eventually disowned her." He looked down at his feet and sighed. "I tried to help her. I really did. I'd send her to rehab, and she'd be fine for a while, then she'd slide right back. Street drugs, prescription drugs, booze…anything she could use to make herself numb. I paid to keep Zach in private schools so he didn't have to face the reality of her addiction, but of course, he knew something was wrong."

Blake looked up at Amanda. He could see his own pain reflected in her eyes. But no one could help him bear his guilt. "I really thought the last facility was the charm. She came out after three months in great spirits, looking better than ever. I put her up in a nice apartment in New York and enrolled her in art school. I even moved Zach to a school near the city so he could stay with her on weekends, and they seemed to be doing really well together. I was in Barbados when she called. Zach was skiing in Vermont with the family of one of his school friends, so she was alone.

She started crying about the mess she'd made of her life. Her voice was slurred. I could barely understand her. She sounded drunk, or high. Probably both." He scrubbed his hand down his face. The last thing he wanted to do was relive that night, but Amanda deserved the truth. "I was so frustrated that she'd relapsed *again*. Life was just a never-ending roller-coaster ride with her, and I was fed up with it. I didn't want to listen to her self-pity or her apologies."

He'd never told anyone about that phone call. "All I could think about while she rambled on was that we'd have to get Zach into a new school and find another rehab center for her. Finally, I told her to go sleep it off. She started crying harder. I told her I didn't want to hear it, and then I hung up on her." He stopped, swallowing the sadness. "The cleaning staff found her body the next day, sprawled across the bed with a pile of empty pill bottles on the nightstand and an empty bottle of vodka on the floor. The girl who loved Christmas died at Christmastime. They ruled it accidental, but I think she was saying 'goodbye,' and I was too selfish and stupid to realize it."

Amanda made a strangled sound of pity. "You couldn't have known that, Blake. Poor Zach...that's why you want him to have a good Christmas this year."

He gave her a halfhearted grin. "I have to try. She loved him more than anything in the world. Tiffany was like a child herself so he adored her." Blake closed his eyes, and he could hear her laughter. "All she ever wanted was for the people around her to be happy. She wanted to be loved."

He stopped, realizing that's exactly what Amanda has said about Zach. He wanted to be loved. Was that why Tiffany had named Blake as guardian? Because she thought he'd understand?

"The next thing I know, the lawyers are telling me I'm responsible for a little boy. I tried to get my brother to take Zach, but my sister-in-law, Michaela, didn't want him living with her precious little girls, as if Tiffany's problems were contagious. They agreed to keep him this summer because I was traveling, but no longer than that. My father won't even acknowledge his existence. So here I am, arguing with you over a kid I barely know. And it's my fault that I don't know him. I haven't even tried. Goddamn it, I failed them both."

He blew out a long, tortured breath. Unshed tears stung his eyes. Now Amanda knew what a complete loser he was. A man who couldn't love his own sister enough to save her. She was silent, then finally just shook her head.

"You didn't fail Tiffany. Your sister was an addict. You can't *make* an addict quit. You can't *wish* them sober. You gave Tiffany the tools, but she didn't use them. You were raised to think kindness was a sign of failure, and in spite of that you were still kind to Tiffany. You tried to protect her and Zachary. And you took care of Zach when she couldn't. That's not failure. That's love."

That's love.

His heart pounded hard against his chest. He didn't believe in love anymore. Did he? He could hear Tiffany's laughter in the air again, and he closed his eyes. It was crazy, but he could smell the ocean, hear her giggles as she ran ahead of him. He always let her win those races, just to see her joy. Amanda squeezed his hands again, and he looked up at the woman who was doing far more than rebuilding his house. She was redesigning his entire life.

"I loved my sister." The words felt heavy and warm on his lips.

"Yes, and you'll love Zach, too. You know how I know?"

He looked into her bright blue eyes and shook his head, unable to speak.

"Blake, the person you just described to me *is* Zachary. He has his mother's sense of fun and adventure. And he really cares about people. He's been so kind to me…" Her voice drifted off. Blake remembered Zach's words. *She cries so much... She has nightmares.* Zach had been taking care of Amanda. Just like Tiffany would have.

He stood, pulling Amanda to her feet in front of him. He put his hands gently on either side of her face. She stared up at him, looking uncertain.

"It's still there, isn't it?" he whispered. How was that possible? "This thing between us, even after all this. It's still there."

She nodded, suddenly solemn. He slowly dropped his head and brushed his lips against hers. He didn't go further until he felt her hands sliding into his hair. With that unspoken invitation, he pressed into her and tasted everything he'd been missing for these desperately long days. Sweet Jesus, it was even better than he remembered. She was warm and intoxicating, sweet and dangerous. He wrapped his arms around her waist and pulled her up off her feet without moving his mouth from hers, wanting to consume her. All the emotion of the past few hours ignited in this kiss. When he finally set her down, it was with a groan of frustration. Kisses were no longer going to be enough with this woman.

Chapter Eleven

Amanda couldn't think. Blood pounded through her veins and a hot flush spread across her skin. Her entire body trembled like a tuning fork.

Blake stared down at her, looking just as ravaged as she felt. His hair was mussed from where she'd had her fingers in it. His dark eyes were nearly black now. She knew her eyes reflected the same desire, so she closed them, terrified of what he might see. This wasn't her. Her chest tightened. Blake was turning her into a different person, and she was so far out of her carefully constructed comfort zone that she couldn't think straight. She shuddered.

"Amanda…" His voice was soft and deep, and her heart raced at the sound of it. "It's okay. Take a deep breath and relax. We'll figure this out together."

"I can't…" She backed out of his arms and away from the heady scent of him so she could think. "I don't know how to do this. I don't even know what 'this' is. It's too much…" The stress of the past few weeks crashed over her like an icy wave, and she felt new tears spilling from her eyes.

Blake brushed the teardrops from her cheeks. She wanted to shove him away, and she wanted to bury her fingers in his hair again and kiss him long and deep. The corner of his mouth twitched up into a crooked grin as if he could read her mind. Then he grew serious.

"You're exhausted." He shook his head. "And it's my fault. I should have come home as soon as I knew Zach was here. But I was afraid of being here with you." He grinned at her surprise. "That's right, sweetheart, you're not the only one who's confused by all of this energy between us. I'm the guy who doesn't believe in romance, and you're the girl who's terrified to try it. I don't know if that makes us the perfect couple or a recipe for disaster." His hands rested lightly on her shoulders. "We'll slow things down a bit, okay? I'm willing to try if that's what you need. Can you help me get to know my nephew better? I really need your help with that."

Her panic faded as she stared into his coffee-colored eyes. He'd opened his heart to her, and she had a feeling that didn't happen very often. Slowly, she returned his smile.

"Friends is a good place to start." She broke the gaze and looked out over the water. She could hear music. She frowned. It was loud rock music.

"Speaking of your nephew, where is he?"

He shrugged. "He's doing his homework."

"That's *what* he's doing. I asked *where* he was."

"He asked to use the living room. Why?"

Amanda started to laugh. "Oh, you've got a lot to learn about little boys. Of course he asked to use the living room. Because he knows that *I* wouldn't have allowed it. Hear that?" She tilted her head toward the sounds rising from the room two stories below them.

"The music?"

"Your living room is now home to two flat-screen televisions, Blake. And the music system. And the game consoles. That sounds like *Guitar Gods* to me. *Not* homework." She tapped her finger lightly on the tip of his nose and giggled when his eyes went wide. "You just got played by a ten-year-old, Uncle Blake." She spun on her heel and headed for the stairs.

Blake helped her put away the painting supplies and ladder after they got Zachary settled in the solarium to do his homework away from the temptation of any state-of-the-art electronics. Once they made sure he had his books open, she gave Blake a tour of the work that had been accomplished while he was gone.

She was proud of how the magnificent old house looked, but Blake was quiet as she showed him around. His only display of emotion was a crooked smile when he saw the iron chandeliers sporting their fresh coat of shiny paprika paint. Three Persian silk rugs divided the large main hall into a trio of distinct spaces, with the formal dining table occupying one end, a sitting area in front of the fireplace, and another near the library.

Blake's future office was still very much a construction zone, with floor-to-ceiling bookshelves and cabinets being constructed the length of one long wall.

The living room was almost completely furnished. She'd managed to snag an enormous leather sectional off the floor of a design center. Several low-slung chairs sat by the windows, with a game table and chairs on the opposite end of the room. That's where the second flat screen was hanging, set up for video games and movies.

Blake still had nothing to say. He hated it. She was sure he hated all of it.

He stopped abruptly in the doorway of his suite upstairs. The massive bed was now washed with a cream-colored finish. All of the formerly dark wood trim in the room was painted to match the bed. The walls were soft blue, reflecting the lake outside. Blake stood in the middle of the room in stunned silence.

"Say *something*, Blake. You're killing me."

"You painted the bed..." He put his hand on it, then turned with a perplexed look on his face. "I couldn't envision this. But you did."

He went to one of the windows looking out over the lake and ran his hand down the knobby raw silk drapes. Elegant but natural. Rich and rough. Like him. That's why she'd selected the material, but she'd never tell him that. She was still holding her breath when he turned to look at her.

"It's amazing. *You're* amazing."

She almost laughed out loud in relief. "I'm so glad you like it."

He gave her a strange look, then shook his head. "Don't take this the wrong way, Amanda. I knew you had talent, but what you've accomplished here in basically a month is mind-boggling. I should stay here and send *you* to Bali to manage the resort opening. You clearly know how to get things done. And your taste is flawless." He walked over to her and put his hands on her shoulders. Her skin tingled at his touch. "When this house is done, I want to talk to you about doing some redecorating at some of the resorts."

Her mind started to spin. Stay in Gallant Lake and work for Blake. Stay here with Zach. Wasn't that what she wanted? But that kiss...

"We can talk about that later." She needed time to process everything. "Right now, Zach needs dinner so we can get him to bed. It's a school night."

"Yes, Mom."

She swatted at him and he ducked, laughing. He spun her by the shoulders and nudged her toward the door.

Chapter Twelve

Amanda leaned against one of the two stone pillars flanking the driveway, wishing she'd grabbed a jacket before coming down to meet Zach's bus. It was almost November, and the air was chilly and damp.

Blake had been back at Halcyon for a couple weeks now, and they were settling into a comfortable routine. They kept their relationship professional during the day, and carefully platonic outside of work hours. They made it work by making Zach their priority. It took a while for uncle and nephew to really warm up to each other. Zach resented his uncle's arrival. Not only because of the argument he'd witnessed, but because he felt Blake betrayed Zach by sending him away, first to Blake's brother, then to boarding school. At least, that's what Zach told the school counselor. The counselor recommended Blake give Zach time to start trusting. That Blake would have to earn it.

It was sports that had finally broken the ice a few days earlier. When Amanda showed them Zach's redecorated room, complete with pinstripes and life-size decals of his favorite athletes on the wall, Blake was almost as excited as Zach was. Amanda tried explaining her paint and curtain choices, and realized they weren't even listening. They were busy studying a poster of the home football team, debating their chances in the play-offs this year.

During dinner in the solarium that night, the two moved on from football to discover more things they had in common. They liked the same computer games. They liked *Star Wars* and *Star Trek* and anything else that started with *star*.

And they both loved her dark chocolate cake. Zach was still wary of Blake, but at least they were talking.

Blake worked from his office at the resort every day while Zach was in school and Amanda was supervising the work at Halcyon. Then he'd help his nephew with homework while Amanda prepared dinner. The three of them would gather in the living room after the meal for television, a movie, video games or a hotly contested game of cards.

Once Zach was in bed, Amanda and Blake would watch television or read before retiring to their rooms. Conversation was usually at a minimum when they were alone together, but their time was still comfortable and relaxed, except for that pesky sexual tension that always made her heart race in his presence.

There was still some work to be done at Halcyon, but it was on hold while the cherry wood needed for Blake's office was on back order. In the meantime, Bobby's crew was working on the outside of the house, ripping up the overgrown shrubbery and beginning repairs to the old fountain. Today they were up the hill, working on the old carriage house, now a garage.

She was glad to have them out of the house for a while. Especially that one guy, Russ. He put her on edge. It felt like he was *watching* her all the time. No one was allowed to smoke inside, but the room always reeked of cigarettes when he was in there. Maybe that's why she took such a dislike to the man—he reminded her of the guy who'd assaulted her in the city. She shook off that train of thought with a shudder.

She was still fighting off little panic attacks, although she'd been better since Blake's return. The nightmares were less frequent, but not gone. With all this stress, starting any kind of relationship with Blake right now would have been a bad idea. Besides, Zachary needed a stable home, free from drama. That was why she'd begged Blake to dial it back. It was the right thing to do.

He wasn't making it easy to ignore the sizzling energy between them, though, making a habit of appearing at odd times throughout the day. She'd turn around from cleaning the grout in the solarium, and find him standing in the doorway, watching her with that crooked grin. She and Bobby would spread the plans for the office on the dining table to determine what to do next, and suddenly Blake would be leaning over the table with them, discussing the options. He'd stand so close she could feel the heat from his body, but he was careful not to touch her. She'd be sipping her morning coffee on the veranda, and there he'd be, steaming mug in hand, joining her silently to watch the autumn sun rise above Gallant Lake. She wasn't sure if he was testing *her* willpower or his own, but she had no doubt the seemingly casual appearances were very intentional.

The rumble of the school bus broke her reverie. When Zach saw her standing there, he started waving before the bus even stopped. He jumped off with a football clutched tightly in his hands. Several boys shouted goodbyes to him as the bus pulled away.

"Miss Amanda! Look, Kyle gave me his old football so I can practice with it!" Zach held it up for her to admire, which she did while giving him a quick hug. He squirmed away, but not until she'd held him for a few seconds.

"A football? That's awesome, Zach!"

"You wanna see how I can throw?"

She laughed at his eager expression. "Sure! I'll run up the driveway and you throw me the ball!"

She caught his first pass with ease. She tossed it back and ran farther up the driveway as he followed. Rain from earlier in the week left the center of the circular drive wet near the fountain, with a huge puddle of standing water at the edge of the paving stones.

When Zach threw the next pass, it veered to the side. All those childhood memories of playing touch football with the neighborhood kids came flooding back to her. She kept her eye on the ball and leaped for it. Her fingers wrapped around the ball and brought it down, but she lost her footing.

And landed with a splash in the midst of the muddy water.

Blake was chatting casually with Jamal in the surveillance room as they reviewed some of the new camera locations at Halcyon that had been added to the resort's security feed. Jamal cleared his throat and grew serious.

"I was talking to Julie yesterday, and she said some of the employees are being harassed around town."

He stiffened. *"What?"*

"Julie had some guy ask her if she worked here. When she said yes, he spat at her feet and called her a money whore, then took off."

"Jesus…"

"Yeah. A few other employees have reported incidents, too. And in the past couple of weeks, we've had some cars vandalized in the employee lot. Key scratches and crap like that."

"And you're looking into it?" Jamal gave a sharp nod.

"I've got Tim doing some recon around town to see if he can ID the guys. Julie didn't recognize him. We brought the deputy sheriff into the loop, and he's on it, too."

"Oh, great." Sheriff Dan, who grew up in Gallant Lake, wasn't a fan of his casino plans.

"Dan's good people, Blake. He doesn't want this kind of trouble in town." Blake looked at the camera feeds coming from Halcyon, and Jamal rushed to reassure him. "The so-called preservation society swears it's not one of theirs. We're keeping a tight eye on the house. The new cameras will help."

On one of the monitors, Blake saw Zach jump off the
school bus, running toward Amanda. Their quick, tight
embrace was such a simple thing. Such a moment of very
normal, everyday joy for a little boy. Blake had never in
his life ridden on a school bus. He'd never been greeted at
home like that. Amanda was right. Zach needed this. It was
everything Tiffany wanted for her boy.

Amanda took off running and disappeared from the
view of the gate camera. Then Zach threw the football.
Jamal was watching the same action, and he tapped a few
keys to switch the view to the feed from the cameras on the
front of Halcyon, looking down the driveway.

Amanda was running, her eyes firmly on a well-thrown
football. He could see what was going to happen, but there
was nothing he could do to warn her. She leaped for the ball
and fell into about five inches of muddy water. He held his
breath until she sat up, unhurt, her ponytail hanging down
her back in a soggy mess. And clutching the football in
her hands. He couldn't stop from laughing out loud, and
Jamal chuckled, too.

Zach was running up to Amanda now, and even without sound it was easy to see he was laughing hysterically.
He dropped to the driveway and howled with glee, arms
wrapped around his stomach as Amanda sat there in the
water eyeing him. She held out her hand for Zach to help
her up. He stood and walked over.

"Don't do it, Zach!" Blake and Jamal both called out at
the same time. Even from that distance, they could read
Amanda's expression and body language.

Zach couldn't leave her there. He couldn't see this dam-
sel in distress was plotting revenge. As soon as she clasped
Zach's hand, Amanda yanked him into the puddle along-
side her. Water and mud went flying when he landed on his
hands and knees. He sat up and looked like he was sputter-
ing. Not satisfied, Amanda smacked the heel of her hand

onto the water and splashed Zach. They were both laughing now, and Zach splashed her back. Amanda tackled him into the thick mud at the edge of the water. He grabbed a handful of mud and rubbed it into her face. Blake winced and laughed out loud again.

Those two were having too much fun. In a mud puddle. Something else Blake had never done. A memory of Tiffany came back to him in a rush, which had been happening a lot these past few weeks. Tiffany was about Zach's age in this particular memory, and she was dancing on the back terrace of their house on Long Island in the pouring rain. Her long dark hair clung to her skin, her clothes were drenched, and still…she danced. He could hear her laughing voice, begging him to join her. But he didn't. He was too afraid of what his father would have said.

There wasn't a doubt in his mind that his vivacious sister would have been right there in the mud today with Amanda and Zach. He watched as they scrambled for the now slimy football. Eventually they both got to their feet, still laughing and wrestling with each other. That's when Blake identified one of the emotions coursing through him. He was envious.

He was envious of these two people finding that much joy in a mud puddle. He was envious of Zach being able to hear Amanda's pealing laughter while Blake watched a silent monitor. He was envious of Amanda planting a big, muddy kiss on Zach's face. He was even more envious of Zach for receiving that kiss. He stood abruptly and left the room without saying a word to Jamal.

He needed to get to Halcyon.

Chapter Thirteen

Amanda and Zach climbed the stone stairway laughing and gasping for breath. She couldn't remember the last time she'd laughed this hard. It wasn't until they reached the door that she realized they had a dilemma.

They were covered in mud and dripping wet. They couldn't go inside like this. Not across those newly polished marble floors and hand-knotted silk rugs. Amanda pressed her lips together. That's what she got for cavorting in the mud like a teenager. She looked at Zach.

"Okay. We need to get you into a bathtub, but I don't want to bring this mess in the house. Take off your shoes and socks and leave them out here. I'll run and get some towels from the laundry room and I'll be right back to wrap you up and get you upstairs. Okay?"

Zach nodded with a shiver. She should have been more practical and kept him out of the puddle. She toed off her muddy sneakers and rolled up her jeans.

"I'll be right back—stand close to the building to stay out of the wind, okay?"

"I'm cold, Miss Amanda."

"I know—I'll hurry." Amanda wrung the water out of her ponytail—she must have looked a sight—and dashed into the house. She ran to the laundry room next to the kitchen, grabbed two big towels and ran back into the main hall. She slid to a stop when Blake walked through the front door with Zach in his arms. *Uh-oh.* Surely Randall men didn't believe in playing in the mud. She braced herself for a scolding.

But wait—he was grinning. He winked at her as he walked by. *Winked!*

"I'll take care of this little mud puppy. You get yourself into a hot shower, Miss Amanda."

"But your clothes..." He was holding the filthy little boy against his white dress shirt and gray pants. The shirt was surely ruined. Zach looked up at Blake mischievously and slapped his hand against Blake's cheek, leaving a perfect muddy handprint. Amanda couldn't hold back her giggle.

"Nice," Blake said with resignation. "It's a little late to worry about clothes at this point. You both need to get clean, warm and dry. Upstairs. Now." His words were demanding, but his brown eyes were twinkling with humor. She threw a towel around Zach and draped the other around herself to catch the dripping water as she followed them upstairs.

Steam wrapped around her in the shower and she sighed as her body warmed up again. When she stepped out to dry herself, she could hear Blake and Zachary laughing in Zach's room next door. She could only imagine what *that* bathroom was going to look like when they were done. The deep timbre of Blake's laughter made her skin tingle as she pulled on a fresh pair of jeans and a sweater. He stopped by her room and called through the door that he and Zach were headed down to the living room, and he was going to light a fire. She told him she'd join them shortly.

But first, Zach's bathroom.

She got on her hands and knees by the bathtub and scrubbed the remaining dirt from the sides. Blake may have cleaned the boy, but he was predictably blind to the mess he left behind. She reached across to wipe down the far side before rinsing it one last time.

There was a sharp intake of breath behind her. Blake stood in the doorway. His clean shirt was still unbuttoned, leaving a wide swath of chest exposed. She forced her eyes away from that sight to make eye contact. But *his* eyes were focused elsewhere. They were fixed on her behind, which, from his angle, must have been quite a sight with her in this position. She blushed and sat back on her heels quickly. His eyes flickered to hers.

"Hey, you just ruined my view." He grinned and tipped his head toward the door. "Come down and enjoy the heat from the fireplace. We have staff to clean bathrooms. Although I may rethink that after the sight I just had…"

She threw the sponge at him playfully and turned on the water to rinse the soap away.

"You're such a diva, Blake. How did you ever become so successful in the hotel business when you can't even clean up after yourself?" She held out her hand for him to help her up. He ignored her question and asked one of his own.

"Isn't this how Zach met his fate outside? Helping you to your feet?"

He read her confusion and laughed as he pulled her up to stand directly in front of him.

"Security cameras. I was in the surveillance room."

"They're watching us from the resort?" She knew there were cameras, but it never occurred to her that someone was sitting around watching her.

"Relax. Exterior views only—the entrances and the gate. Today's episode of *Life at Halcyon* was highly entertaining." He was looking at her intensely now, a look that didn't match the playfulness of his voice. The air evaporated from her lungs when he slid his arm around her back and pulled her close, brushing her damp hair away from her face with his other hand. His fingers lingered on her cheek. "Actually, I find everything you do to be highly entertaining."

Since his return, they'd carefully avoided touching each other. It was all a wonderfully played performance. But now they were too close. He smelled like soap and something intoxicating. She found herself leaning into him rather than pulling away. Unbidden, her hands rested on his forearms, then slowly slid up past his shoulders, stopping with her fingers behind his broad neck. He stared at her silently, waiting for her to decide what would happen next. With a groan of surrender she pulled him down to her mouth. She wanted this. She needed it. Right now.

He let out his breath with a growl and his mouth fell on hers hungrily. Their tongues met and danced and twisted, and she was every bit as aggressive as he was. He pulled her hips into his. She not only allowed it to happen, she ground her lower body against his and felt a thrill when he hardened against her. She'd lost control of herself, and for once in her life, she didn't care. He pulled his mouth away from hers, dropping quick kisses on her cheeks, her eyelids, her hair, her chin. Then he took her mouth again and she clung to his shoulders. She felt like she was falling, and she was. She was falling for him. This was uncharted territory, and a surge of panic rose.

He sensed it immediately and pulled away, leaving his hands on her hips to keep her upright. She had no doubt that if he let go of her, she'd crumple at his feet in a boneless heap. They stood there, panting, staring at each other. Every kiss seemed to leave them in this same position. His hooded eyes were deepest dark mahogany, his voice gruff and tight.

"I won't apologize for how much I want you, Amanda."

Instead of the normal dread that thought should invoke, she realized she wanted him, too. She wanted to defeat *all* of her demons and she wanted this man to help her do it.

He gave her one last gentle kiss on the lips. "We should go. The fire's lit, Zach's waiting to beat us both at *Guitar Gods*, and I ordered a pizza from the village."

Amanda followed him in thoughtful silence. Is this what life could be like at Halcyon? Or was it just a teasing glimpse of something she'd never be a part of?

* * *

Blake looked down at Amanda sleeping in the big chair. He'd pulled the chair closer to the fire earlier, and she'd read a book there while he and Zach played a video game. It had been a lovely family evening. Another first for Blake.

There'd been no pizza nights in his childhood. No mud fights. No women cleaning bathtubs in snug jeans that made their ass look like a perfect heart. He didn't realize how much he'd been missing until right this very moment.

Zach had gone up to bed, and was probably fast asleep already. Blake dropped to his knees in front of Amanda's reclining form and brushed a golden curl away from her face. She stirred and opened her eyes dreamily. Stretching like a cat, she sighed and smiled at him. It was a smile of contentment and security. Of innocence and anticipation. More than anything else in the world, he wanted to see that smile on her face every day for the rest of his life. The thought was unfamiliar and sobering, but truer than anything he'd felt before. This woman made him think about forever. That wall around his heart was shattering, leaving him frighteningly vulnerable.

She sat up and grew more serious. Was she worrying about that bathroom kiss? She stood and they faced each other, not touching, tension filling the space between them.

He bit back a frustrated curse and put his hands on her shoulders. Then he did what he thought he had to do. He lied.

"Nothing has changed, Amanda." He didn't know about her, but *everything* had changed for him. Still, he told her what she needed to hear. "We'll take things at your pace. It won't be easy after that kiss, but we're adults, and we can handle this." He pressed his lips against her forehead and felt her body tense. He was missing a piece of her story. This reaction of hers was from more than being mugged. He lifted his head and waited quietly until she raised her eyes to his. "What is it, baby? What happened to make you so frightened? Who hurt you?"

She shook her head quickly, pulling away from him. Her clear eyes grew cloudy with tension. Then she drew her shoulders back and gave him that brave, but false, smile. She was burying her fears again.

He tried one more time. "Tell me what it is. Let me help you…"

"I'm fine. I'm good. Just tired. Good night, Blake." Without another word, she turned and headed up the staircase. He followed in silence, watching her close the door to her room without looking back at him once.

He stood in front of his bedroom windows for a long time. Gallant Lake was bathed in the soft light of a nearly full moon, but he had no appreciation for the view. All he could think of was the troubled woman getting ready for bed next door. He distracted himself by checking his email and responding to a few questions from his resort managers in various locations. Work was his comfort zone, somewhere he felt sure of himself and in control. Two things he never felt when he was in Amanda Lowery's presence.

He finally stood and stretched, ready to attempt sleep at last. Walking over to the fireplace, he stared at an old painting of Halcyon on the mantel as he unbuttoned his shirt. He couldn't shake the feeling that something was wrong in this house tonight. He was sitting on the edge of the bed removing his shoes when he heard the first scream.

She has nightmares…

Amanda!

He ran into the hallway, wearing nothing but his jeans. Zach was just coming out of his room at the opposite end of the hall with wide eyes. Blake ran to her door and grabbed the knob. Locked. Another terror-filled scream shuddered through the hallway. He didn't hesitate. A well-placed kick splintered the wood next to the lock and the door flew open.

She was thrashing under the sheets, her face soaked with tears.

"Get off me! Stop!"

"Amanda! Wake up, it's just a dream." Blake grabbed her shoulders. She tried to hit him so he took both of her hands and held them over her head with one of his. His upper body was over hers, pinning her down. "Open your eyes! Look at me!"

Her eyes flashed open at his demand. So much stark fear staring back at him. As she began to focus, her breathing slowed, but she was still shaking all over. She tried to move her hands, but he had them captured above her. Her face paled.

"Please don't…that's how he…"

He released her immediately and slid off her. He held one of her hands in his and sat on the edge of the bed. She took in a ragged breath. "Zach?"

Blake turned and saw Zach frozen in the doorway.

"Go back to bed, buddy. It was just a bad dream. I'll take care of Miss Amanda."

Zach looked from Blake to Amanda, and she gave him a nod of reassurance. He hesitated, then turned away. When they heard his bedroom door close, Blake let out a long breath.

"Jesus, Amanda." He brushed a strand of hair away from her face. "Why didn't you tell me this was happening?" He felt a stab of guilt for not asking her about them before now. She was right—he dealt with problems he didn't know how to solve by ignoring them.

She pushed herself up, and he quickly propped pillows behind her so she could lean back against the headboard, curls tumbling around her shoulders. Her pale blue cotton nightgown was damp with her sweat and clung to her. Her breathing was rough and uneven, her cheeks wet with tears. What was left of that wall around his heart came tumbling down with a thundering crash. Finally exposed, he could actually feel his heart breaking for her.

"You broke my door." She sounded so forlorn.

"Yes, I did. And I'll do it again. No more locks."

She shook her head emphatically, but he caught and cupped her chin in his hand. "No more nightmares behind locked doors, Amanda."

He turned so he could lean against the headboard next to her, then pulled her close. Her arms wrapped tightly around his torso, and she felt soft and sweet in his embrace. He kissed her hair as she rested her head on his chest. She was so quiet he thought she'd fallen asleep.

"I was sixteen." When she spoke, a chill fell over the room. He held his breath, wondering if she'd continue. Maybe she was talking in her sleep.

"I was sixteen," she started again with a stronger voice, definitely awake. "And you were right, I *was* a high school cheerleader. Jimmy Waldron was our quarterback. The team was undefeated that season, and Jimmy was the hero of Jenner, Kansas. He was a senior. So handsome. So popular. And he asked *me* to the homecoming dance. I couldn't believe it. I wore my first long dress…it was yellow. I'd always been a tomboy, you know, climbing trees and playing softball, but that night I felt like a princess."

He pulled the blanket up and wrapped it around her. He imagined her as a teenager, dressed in a sun-colored gown, with her wavy blond hair falling down her back. As pretty as the image was, he already knew this story was not going to have a happy ending.

"Jimmy said he had a surprise for me after the dance. He drove me out to the river in his truck. There was a full moon that night." Her voice was flat, and she paused after each sentence as if she was summoning the courage to say the next one. "I thought that's why he took me there. To see the moon over the water. He kissed me. My first kiss.

But then…" She stopped talking for so long that he thought she might not continue. He wasn't about to push her. "He… grabbed at me. I got scared, and he got rough. He pushed me to the ground and I just lay there staring up at him. I didn't run away. I didn't even try to. I was so stupid…"

"Don't say that. It wasn't your fault." Blake's throat was tight. "You did nothing wrong."

She kept talking, as if she couldn't stop herself from reciting the story she'd been reliving in nightmares. "He tore my dress. Everything he did hurt me…"

His stomach churned.

"You don't have to tell me…"

But apparently she did.

"He held my hands over my head and…" Blake closed his eyes tightly, trying to block the image of what she was describing. "I thought I was going to die. I begged him to stop. There was a stone under my left shoulder. A really sharp stone. I still have a little scar where it cut into me while he…while he…" She took a deep breath. "He kept saying I *wanted* it. But I didn't. I *didn't!* I finally just focused on that stone cutting into my back. I didn't think about anything but that damned stone…"

"Amanda…" His voice broke.

"By the time he dropped me off at home, I was numb."

"You were in shock, baby," Blake whispered into her hair. "He's in prison now?"

She shook her head against his chest. "Last I heard, he was selling used cars in Wichita."

"He wasn't charged?" How could that bastard be walking around free after raping her?

"It was…complicated. That's the word my stepfather used. You see, Jimmy's father was the mayor of our little town. He also owned the car dealership. My stepdad, Mitch, worked for him. My mom *wanted* to call the police, but Mitch didn't want me to cause any trouble…"

"And your mom dropped it, just like that?"

"She'd come hold me when I had nightmares, but she wouldn't go against Mitch, not even for me. I hated her for that weakness. He left her a few years after that for some woman he sold a car to."

Blake squeezed her tightly. He tried to imagine a young girl coming home torn and bloodied and in shock. What kind of man could see her like that and not call the police? But he knew. He knew his own father probably would have reacted the same way. Don't cause trouble. Don't damage the family reputation. Don't look weak.

She gave a short, mirthless laugh. "You know what Mitch was worried about? He said if I caused trouble for Jimmy while the football team was headed for the state championship, the whole town would hate us. And they *did* win the state championship. I always thought that trophy should have been mine. They wouldn't have had it without me staying quiet."

He swallowed hard, not knowing what to say to that. "Did you at least change schools?"

"We would have had to move, and Mitch wouldn't do that. He let me stay home until the bruises healed, and then I had to go back to class. It was just pure luck that I didn't end up pregnant or infected with something. But the girl I was died that day. The guys on the football team snickered when I walked by. The whole school was talking. By Christmas, I'd dropped my friends, or they'd dropped me—I don't really know which. I didn't trust anyone or anything." She fidgeted in his arms, restless and tense. "I couldn't stand to be touched after that. So much worse than I am now. Every man's touch felt like his hands."

Blake ran his hand slowly up and down her arm, stunned into silence. He kissed the top of her head again, then tipped her chin up so he could look at her face. Her eyes were sad and bright with tears, and the sight made his heart tighten.

"You've been having nightmares this bad all these years?"

"No. I locked it all away for a long time once I left Kansas. I had some counseling in college to deal with my fear of being touched. I built my career. I even dated a little. But being touched…like that…has always been a problem." He felt her tremble. "I went back to counseling a year ago. Dr. Jackson insisted I talk about the rape in session, which brought it all back, and that's when the nightmares and panic attacks started up again. She said it's healthy in a way, because I'm finally confronting my past. When I'm stressed, it's so much worse."

"But Dr. Jackson thinks you'll work through it?"

"God, I hope so." She smiled for the first time, and Blake kissed her forehead in relief. It was amazing anyone could smile after what she'd gone through. "She said I pushed the whole thing so deeply into denial for so long that I'm paying the price now, by having this hyperreaction to it. But she insists I have to confront my past before I can move on. Being raped ended my childhood. But I can't let it be the end of me."

Her voice faded at the end of the sentence, as if she wasn't quite convinced. He thought back to that first day they'd met. How she'd tried to keep him from touching her. When she'd landed on the hard stone floor and he'd been above her, she'd passed out from terror. Now he knew why. He couldn't imagine the toll that would take on a person as years passed. He looked down at her.

"Thank you, Amanda."

Her forehead crinkled. "For what?"

"For telling me. That couldn't have been easy."

She rested back against his chest. He put his hand protectively on the back of her head, cradling her, ready to fight off the whole damned world for her.

"It just came out. I've only talked to my cousins about it.

And Dr. Jackson, of course. Did I tell you that in my dreams, I always fight back? The doctor says that's important— something about reclaiming my power. She keeps encouraging me to talk about it more. She says it will help me accept it so I can move forward. But it's…hard to talk about. It takes a lot out of me… I get so tired…"

And just like that, her breathing changed, and Blake knew she'd fallen into a deep sleep. He carefully slid down onto the bed with her and held her against him, watching her face as she slept.

Some deep, unnamed emotion began to blossom in his heart as he watched her breathe in and out softly. He didn't know what it was, and it frightened him. He placed his lips softly on her forehead, then pulled her closer as he closed his eyes.

Chapter Fourteen

Blake slipped out of Amanda's room before she woke. Leaving her soft, warm body was more difficult than he'd expected, and he almost crawled right back under the covers. He stood next to the bed for a long time, watching how the early morning light kissed her face, with her hair fanned across the pillow.

He wanted to make sure she never had another sad moment in her life. *Ever.* And that realization was what propelled him out of her room. These roiling, unfamiliar emotions scared the hell out of him.

He was a coward for showering and leaving for the resort before she came downstairs for breakfast, but he didn't know what to do. He'd never felt this way about a woman in his entire life. In his world, women chased after *him*, and for all the wrong reasons. They wanted his lifestyle, his wealth and, yes, he supposed they liked his looks, too. But none of them really knew who he was.

His whole life was just one unending example of how relationships never worked. His parents. His brother and Michaela. He and the few women he'd tried getting serious with. Tiffany and every loser she'd brought home. The Randall family seemed genetically incapable of long-term relationships.

He stopped pacing his office and headed down to the lobby, restless inside and out. Amanda knew what Tiffany's death had done to him. She knew his fears about Zachary, and she loved his nephew fiercely. She knew his secrets, and after last night, he knew hers. Did that mean they had a relationship? Did he want that? Did *she*? Would theirs be just as doomed as every other relationship he'd had?

His attraction to her made no sense at all. She was petite and blonde, while he generally preferred tall and exotic. She was vulnerable, and he'd never liked weakness of any kind. She challenged him, and he generally had no patience for people who did that.

But she had ocean-blue eyes he could easily drown in. Curves that whispered his name every time she came near him. Lips softer than velvet. He scrubbed both hands down his face with a groan. He was driving himself crazy.

"What was that, Mr. Randall?" Julie's question jolted him back to awareness. He'd been so lost in his thoughts he hadn't even noticed she'd walked over to join him near the center of the lobby.

"Nothing, Julie. I'm just tired."

She tipped her head thoughtfully. "Yes, you've been busy since your return to Gallant Lake. Is everything all right?" Then she came right out and asked it. "Are you happy with everything Amanda did at Halcyon?"

He gave her a hard look. She was asking about more than the renovation of the house. Amanda hadn't had many champions in her life, and he was glad Julie was one of them. The corner of his mouth lifted in a crooked grin.

"Yes, Julie, I'm happy with *everything* Amanda has done at Halcyon."

Her shoulders visibly relaxed. "Good. She's working so hard to make that place a home. Zach's a great kid. We'd all miss him if he had to leave. And Amanda—"

"Neither of them will be leaving." Not if he had anything to do with it.

"Oh! Well, that's good news."

She saw something she didn't like near the front door and frowned at one of the doormen. He caught her expression and jumped to attention, looking around frantically for the infraction. He finally saw the crumpled piece of discarded paper on the floor and scooped it up, disposing of it. He glanced back for Julie's approval. Blake bit back a smile. When the general manager retired that coming winter as planned, Blake couldn't imagine anyone other than Julie taking the job. She ran a tight ship.

A silver Rolls-Royce came to a stop in front of the front doors, which were propped open on this crisp but sunny morning.

"Is it just me," Blake asked, "or are there an unusual number of very expensive cars rolling up to the resort this morning?"

Julie nodded, glancing at the two clerks manning the busy reception desk. "Yes. The entire west wing is booked with guests for the Fitzgerald wedding tomorrow. Very upscale. A lot of guests are arriving today from the city."

"How'd we land something that big?" Blake watched a silver-haired woman stride through the front doors draped in a fur cape, carrying a tiny dog in her arms. "And when did we start allowing *pets*?"

"Remember that *Times* bridal magazine ad you thought would be a waste of money? Too expensive for a one-time deal?" Julie's voice stayed cool while she kept a sharp eye on the doorman carrying Dog Lady's Louis Vuitton luggage. Blake gave Julie a sharp look and caught the barely perceptible shrug she gave him. "We ran it, and the phones have been busy ever since."

No wonder Julie and Amanda had become friends. They were both smart, sassy women who had no problem challenging him. "We started allowing dogs weighing less than fifteen pounds in August as an experiment. Manhattan socialites love to take their little fashion-accessory doggies everywhere. We only allow them in certain rooms, and guests pay a very large, nonrefundable deposit for the privilege."

There was a time when he would have been furious to find out about these policy changes after the fact. No Surprises Lifestyle and all that. It must be the lack of sleep that was making him so complacent.

"Sounds like you've got everything under control here, Julie. Nice work."

He didn't miss her self-satisfied smile, gone as fast as it had appeared. "Thank you, Mr. Randall. Now, if you'll excuse me, I think I should step in and help at the desk."

"No problem." She started to turn away, but stopped when he rested his hand on her arm. "Julie...thank you for being there for Amanda and Zachary while I was gone."

There was an awkward silence. It was unlike him to be so personal with his employees. Then she patted his hand softly.

"Mr. Randall, it was my pleasure. You're a lucky man to have both of them in your life."

He watched her walk away. There was a time not long ago when he made sure there was a very clear line between his all-consuming business life and barely existent personal life. That line had become increasingly blurred lately.

Amanda busied herself with dinner that evening, trying to determine how she felt about everything that had happened in the last twenty-four hours. The kiss in Zach's bathroom. Blake asking questions about her past she couldn't answer. And then the nightmare, which answered all those questions anyway.

She placed a pot of water on the stove. She'd woken during the night and watched him sleeping next to her. She'd reached out and touched the dark, curling hair on his chest with her fingertips, then pulled away when he moaned and rolled onto his side. He'd wrapped his arm around her and drew her close, and she'd let him. No panic. No fear. His arms felt like a safe place to be. She felt oddly bereft when she woke later and realized he'd left her, and she hadn't seen or heard from him all day. She wasn't even sure he'd show up for the ravioli dinner she was cooking right now.

Did he feel differently now that he knew her past? Would things be weird between them? She chuckled to herself. How much weirder could they be? The two of them continued to dance around each other, pretending to be no more than friends, walking on eggshells unless, of course, they were kissing. When they kissed, they couldn't get enough of each other.

But something was. Ever since the work started in Blake's office, she'd felt this sense of impending...*something*. It wasn't the protesters, although Blake said there'd been a few acts of minor vandalism recently. It wasn't her usual panic-driven imagination. It was deeper than that. For all the joy of watching Blake and Zachary become a family, and whatever was blossoming between her and Blake, it still felt like there was trouble simmering in this house. The kind of trouble that couldn't be blamed on an imaginary ghost.

She was dumping the pasta into the boiling water when her skin warmed and her pulse quickened. She turned to find Blake leaning against the door frame in virtually the same pose he'd used weeks ago when she'd cooked that first meal for him. His eyes sparkled with knowing humor. "I have some very fond memories of this kitchen." He pushed away from the doorway and moved deliberately in her direction. She had a wooden spoon in her hand and ended up holding it between them as if to ward him off. He didn't stop until the spoon was resting lightly against his chest.

"I have to go into the city tomorrow morning for a meeting. I'll be back in time for dinner, but you're not cooking. I'm taking you to Galantè. Just the two of us."

"What about Zach?"

"Jamal's wife, Annie, will stay here with Zach for a few

hours." His face grew serious. "I know we're coming at this whole thing backward and sideways, but now that we've kissed and fought and made up and agreed to be friends and are raising a young child together and sharing our deepest secrets...well, I think it's time for us to have a first date, don't you?"

She chuckled at the absurdity of the relationship he'd just outlined. "Yeah, I guess that would be the logical next step in this entirely illogical relationship."

But a date? A *real* date? That would make this relationship a lot more serious. A lot more real. It would move them a giant step forward, and she wasn't sure she was ready for what that might mean.

Blake put his hand on her cheek and she leaned into it without thinking. It was just the natural thing to do. She closed her eyes as he bent to kiss her softly. He whispered her name, and the kiss quickly deepened to something meaningful and special and intimate. This kiss wasn't about their physical attraction, it was about something *more*, and she knew he felt it, too. It carried a promise of what was to come. He pulled away with a look of frustrated regret and whispered in her ear.

"Wear something pretty tomorrow." And he was gone, calling Zach to dinner as he left the kitchen. She leaned back against the counter, touching her lips with her fingertips. Tomorrow she was going to have a first date with a man who already knew her better than any other.

The following evening, as promised, they were seated together at a small table near the windows in Galantè. He'd asked her to wear something nice, so she'd pulled out a long velvet skirt Mel had sent her last winter. It was dark peacock blue, and flared just enough to dance around her ankles when she walked. The matching satin blouse was styled like a man's oxford shirt, and she'd tied it casually at the waist.

Blake was devilishly handsome in his dark suit and red tie. The flickering candlelight accentuated the strong lines of his face as well as the deep cleft in his chin. He was watching her in obvious amusement.

"What?" She wiped steak sauce from the corner of her mouth with her napkin.

"I'm just wondering where you put it all. Do you have a hollow leg I don't know about?" He was admiring her for *eating*. Terrific. Their waitress swooped in to whisk their dinner plates away and ask if they wanted dessert. Blake nodded.

"We'll share a caramel lava cake, Sarah. And bring two cappuccinos, please."

"Of course, Mr. Randall." And then she was gone. Amanda looked out at the peaceful lake shimmering in the moonlight, shadowed by mountains. "How did you get here?"

"What do you mean?"

"You own hotels in Barbados, Miami, Bali, Las Vegas. What brought you to a little blue-collar town in upstate New York?"

Blake followed her gaze toward the lake, his voice soft and low. "I'm really not sure. One of my advisors saw the resort on the market and did some recon on the viability of putting a casino here. It would be difficult, but not impossible. I liked the idea of something this close to Manhattan. Halcyon was on the market, too, and I figured we'd need the extra land, so I bought a castle."

"How did you get in the resort business in the first place? Were you following your father's footsteps?"

"Hell, no. My great-grandfather started a commercial real estate business—office buildings, mostly—and my grandfather grew it into an empire in New York and New

Jersey." Blake emptied the second bottle of cabernet into their wineglasses and took a sip. "My grandfather died the same year I graduated college. I insisted on taking my portion of the inheritance in cash instead of joining the business, because I knew my father would run it into the ground. Father only agreed because he figured I'd fail and come crawling back."

"But you didn't." She felt a jolt of pride that he had risen to the challenge at such a young age.

"No, I didn't. I bought a struggling hotel in Miami and turned it around. And things just progressed from there. I bought a couple more hotels. I bought the land in Bali where I'm building a resort. And, of course, Gallant Lake."

Sarah brought their dessert to the table, an impressive tower of chocolate cake and caramel sauce topped with whipped cream, nutmeg under a cage of spun sugar.

"What's next?" Amanda asked, picking up her spoon.

"I'm looking at Europe. And I need to do something with this place, just in case the Gallant Lake Preservation Society, or anyone else for that matter, keeps me from building my casino."

She returned his grin. "Julie and I were talking about that last week. This would be a terrific venue for destination weddings, especially if you used Halcyon. It's so close to the city, and…"

"Use Halcyon?" He sat back and looked at her with interest.

She grinned at his confusion. "The house would be a perfect setting for a wedding. Rent out the lawn for outdoor ceremonies and have the receptions out there under tents or here at the resort. You could even rent out the house itself for weddings. That grand staircase would make an amazing entrance for a bride."

"You've really given this some thought."

"I was trying to come up with options to convince you not to tear down the resort."

He was silent, then shook his head.

"I don't want Halcyon to be part of the resort. I want it to be my home."

"I thought you didn't want a home?"

He gave her a crooked grin. The one that always made her heart beat faster. "Zach needs it. And I think I do, too. I'm not worried about the resort. It's smaller than my other properties, but I like the idea of a boutique hotel just outside the city. Between the spa and the new golf course, it'll do just fine."

"Even if you don't get your casino?"

"Is the idea of a casino that could generate hundreds of jobs really that awful?"

"Not awful. Just misguided."

He stood with a chuckle and reached for her hand. "Come on." He rested his hand lightly on her waist and headed for the kitchen. "I want to make a quick check on the wedding reception going on tonight."

The kitchen was a noisy madhouse of activity, but the chef saw them the minute they entered. Dario ignored his employer and rushed up to Amanda, giving her a big kiss on each cheek.

"Eh! My *bambolina*! How are you tonight, *bella mia*? You look so beautiful!"

She laughed and gave him a hug.

"Dario, *mi angelo bello*," she said, "the filet mignon was fantastic. You have to teach me how to make that cognac sauce." He just laughed and shook his finger at her. She knew how tightly the chef protected his recipes. He turned to Blake.

"Signor Randall, you have a treasure in Miss Amanda and your little boy. They make my life brighter here in Gallant Lake."

Blake just nodded, his eyes dark with emotion. "Yes, Dario, they brighten my life, too."

She felt her cheeks flushing. As they walked away, Blake leaned over and spoke softly into her ear.

"My dear Miss Lowery, you seem to have completely charmed my staff. Whatever is your secret?"

She gave him a playful laugh. "I think it's the magic of Halcyon, Mr. Randall."

"Still waiting for Madeleine's ghost to appear up there?"

"What makes you think I haven't already seen her?"

They both laughed. He'd think she was crazy, but sometimes she wondered if there might be something to the legend of Halcyon. What else explained how she and Zach and Blake ended up together in Gallant Lake?

They walked through the kitchen to the long hallway leading to the ballroom, and they could hear the wedding band finishing up a popular line dance. After a smattering of applause, the music slowed. The singer had a beautiful voice, and the song was one of Amanda's favorites.

Blake pulled her close and she tensed out of habit. With her issues about intimacy, slow dancing had never been her thing. He spoke softly, his lips brushing her ear.

"I told you this was a date." His fingers started to move gently across her back, and she began to relax. He started to hum to the music. "What song is this?"

"It's the theme song from one of those silly vampire movies. It's probably the best thing to come from them."

He chuckled. "That's rich coming from a woman who believes in ghosts, don't you think?"

Blake gave her a gentle squeeze, resting his cheek on top of her head and pressing her closer.

Her fear whispered to her from the shadows. What if Blake's feelings for her were just mixed up with the excitement of the house and his new relationship with Zach? If she gave her trust to Blake and he betrayed her, it would break her. She silently prayed that he was different from all the other men in her life.

She finally sighed and focused on the sultry rhythm of the music, letting the warmth of his body push away all fears as they danced together.

Chapter Fifteen

Blake watched Amanda stare pensively into the fire. They'd walked back up to the house in silence after their hallway dance at the resort. Zach was asleep, and Annie said he'd been no problem at all. So Amanda wasn't worried about that. Which left only one thing for her to worry about. *Him.*

"Hey," he said. She swept her eyelashes up and sent him a piercing look. God, her blue eyes slayed him every time. "What's wrong?"

"What do you mean?" Her innocent expression didn't fool him for a minute.

"You seem distracted. What's on your mind?"

She looked down again without answering, staring into the fire. He heard distant music, probably from the wedding reception down the hill.

"Is that piano music coming all the way from the resort?"

Amanda gave him a soft, knowing smile. "Maybe it's courtesy of that ghost you don't believe in."

He knew she was a romantic, but he never thought she was delusional. "Are you telling me you think Madeleine Pendleton is playing a ghostly piano in my house?"

"Maybe she likes music." She caught his expression and laughed softly. "I know it sounds crazy, but sometimes I wonder, you know? The legend had to start somewhere."

The tension on her face earlier was gone as she stared calmly into the fire, which was now crackling merrily. Her profile, with her mane of hair pulled up on top of her head in a messy knot of curls, looked like a Grecian sculpture. Her entire body seemed relaxed and at peace.

If a haunted Halcyon had that effect on her, then he was okay with a haunted Halcyon. If she wanted him to believe in ghosts, then by God, he believed in ghosts. It was that simple. But he wasn't ready to admit it out loud.

"Yeah, the legend came from people who believe in fairy tales. Just because it's a castle doesn't mean it's enchanted."

"Who knows?" Amanda shrugged. "Maybe Madeleine's happy that Halcyon is becoming a home for you and Zach."

"And you." He said the words more forcefully than he'd intended, and she looked at him in surprise.

"Whatever happened to taking things a step at a time?"

He stood and pulled her up with him. "I swear I'm doing my best with the one-step-at-a-time thing. You're already living here at Halcyon." He pressed his lips to her forehead. "I'm not ready to let you go. Not when I'm just learning who you are. You amaze me every freaking day, Amanda, and I don't want to lose you."

Her hands rested lightly on his chest. "You see me *whole*, Blake. I've never seen myself that way. Not since…" Her eyes clouded. "I was broken for so long. But when I'm with you, I feel complete. I'm not afraid. I can't describe it but—"

He silenced her with a kiss. A long, slow, tender kiss. He took his time getting into her mouth and he heard a trembling moan coming from her throat as he explored her. His hands moved down her body and he pulled her close. She didn't pull away this time. He lifted his head and stared into those blue oceans. She whispered that magic word.

"Yes."

That was all he needed to hear. He sat her on the arm of a chair and held up his hand so she knew to wait. She watched in obvious amusement as he rushed to secure the doors and arm the alarm system. Then he led her upstairs to his suite. She hadn't said a word downstairs while he scrambled around. And she still wasn't speaking. Any worries that she was changing her mind vanished when she stopped by the bed and began unbuttoning her blouse.

She reached back to unfasten her skirt after discarding the top. He started to unbutton his shirt, finally yanking it over his head in frantic frustration when her skirt dropped to the floor in a billowing pile of blue-green velvet. He stared at her alabaster skin and all those marvelous curves wrapped in black lace. How could one petite body have that many rounded invitations to please come explore?

His staring must have made her uncomfortable, because she started to raise her hands to cover herself. He stepped forward with an urgent "No" escaping his lips. "The day we met, you said this house was magnificent. But it's not the house. It's you. *You're* the magnificent one, Amanda. Let me drink you in." His voice was raw with desire.

She dropped her hands to her sides, locking her eyes on his as he reached for her. His eyes were going to be her lifeline. He could see that now. It was his job to make sure she felt safe. He held her gaze calmly. He pulled the pins from her hair, brushing it back over her shoulders as it fell.

Flickers of panic danced across her eyes, but they were gone as quickly as they appeared. If he just moved slowly and kept his eyes on hers, they'd be fine. The only problem was he didn't want to go slow. He wanted to devour every inch of her, but he knew he couldn't. Not tonight. His thumbs brushed across her bra and her lips parted with a shuddering sigh. He reached behind her slowly and unhooked the bra, and she let it drop to the floor. His eyes left hers briefly to glance toward the two perfectly rounded breasts now in his hands. His thumbs moved back and forth, and she made a strangled sound deep in her throat. One hand slid lower across her stomach, and she trembled beneath his fingers. But her eyes were fixed on his, and she was trusting him. She groaned as his fingers moved across the slick softness between her legs.

"Blake…" She breathed his name, and he felt his heart catching fire with want of her.

She hissed when his fingers found their target. She didn't look away. Didn't close her eyes. Just stared at him and made the most wonderful little mewling noises in her throat as he explored her. With a small cry, her knees buckled and he caught her up in his arms, laying her on the bed. He finished undressing and crawled on top of her, catching her gaze again. She was nervous, but she nodded, giving him permission. He kissed her deeply, then started trailing kisses down her neck and across her shoulders, glimpsing back up at her face after every other kiss. Her eyes followed him intently. She whimpered softly as he kissed her breasts and teased the tips with his tongue, then his teeth. He started sliding lower with his kisses when she spoke.

"Blake…please… I need you."

That was all he needed to hear. There would be time for exploring later. He grabbed at his nightstand for a condom, then came back over her. She lifted her body up toward his, and he let out a loud groan as he sank slowly into her. Kissing her softly, he watched her eyes grow wide, then fade into blissful, unfocused distraction. Their bodies started moving together. He felt so very absolutely *perfect* inside of her.

This is where he was meant to be. She rocked against him and he pressed into her more firmly, more demanding. There was only one moment when she got tense, and it was when he got distracted watching where their bodies were connected instead of looking at her face. He looked into her eyes and smiled.

"It's me, sweetheart. It's *me* making love to you."

She relaxed again, and they both picked up the pace. He felt her tightening and trembling beneath him. She started whispering his name over and over, and the sound drove him wild.

"It's okay, baby. It's okay to let go."

And she did. She exploded. She opened her mouth to scream and he dropped his mouth over hers to own all of her orgasm before joining her.

Amanda felt like she'd just shattered into a million pieces. So *this* was what it meant to truly make love. She'd had no idea she could feel so powerful and wise and womanly until she felt him coming undone inside of her body. She flexed her fingers against his back and he groaned. He lifted his head from beside hers and propped himself up on one elbow to look down at her. She giggled at the sight of his black hair standing on end.

"Laughter isn't exactly how a man wants to be greeted after mind-blowing sex," he growled at her. But his eyes showed nothing but amusement and heat. Lots of heat. And he'd said "mind-blowing." She grinned.

"You have such terrible bed head." She reached up to run her fingers through his dark curls. He closed his eyes at her touch, and she brought her hand down to his cheek. He leaned into it and sighed.

"I'm still trying to put my *brain* back together, much less my hair. That was... I don't know...*incredible* doesn't even come close to describing it."

"It was my first." She blushed as she said the words. His eyes snapped open, and she wished she'd never said anything.

"Your first?"

"You know...the first time I really...um...finished..."

A lazy smile slid across his face. "I'm honored. How was it?"

She giggled again. "I think you know how it was." Then she turned serious. "Thank you, Blake."

"Oh, hell no, I'm the one who should be down on my knees giving thanks to you, Amanda. It's never, *ever* been that good." He rolled slowly off her to rest on his side and remove the condom, then kissed her softly on the lips. "I want to keep you in my bed forever."

Her breath caught in her throat.

Forever.

"Blake…"

"Shh. Talk later. Not now. Right now I need to sleep, baby. Stay here and sleep with me." He pulled her into his arms and she closed her eyes, feeling safe and at peace.

When Amanda woke, the sun was shining brightly through the windows. She was alone in Blake's bed. She closed her eyes tightly.

She'd made love with Blake Randall. Her client. Zach's uncle. Her "friend." Her date. The man she couldn't imagine living without. She was falling for him, and hard.

The door to the suite opened and he walked in, carrying two mugs of coffee. His hair was damp from a shower, and he was wearing jeans and a plaid shirt with the sleeves rolled up. He looked good enough to eat. She blushed at the thought and pulled the sheets up higher to cover herself, which made him laugh.

"A little late for modesty, don't you think? Your robe is there at the foot of the bed, but feel free to stay as you are." He set a mug on the nightstand.

"I overslept. Zach. Breakfast."

She couldn't form whole sentences in his presence. Blake sat in the big chair by the fireplace, looking annoyingly smug.

"Zach's down at the game room at the resort. Jamal's keeping an eye on him. For some reason, you were in a very deep slumber this morning." Blake laughed when she blushed. "Don't be embarrassed, sweetheart. I managed to feed my nephew breakfast all by myself."

She sat on the edge of the bed, pulled on her robe and reached for the coffee. A dusting of cinnamon covered the white foam at the top of the mug. "And then you trotted into the kitchen and whipped up a cup of Dario's cappuccino? Come clean, Blake. You took Zach to the café at the resort."

He tipped his head back and laughed out loud. She loved the sound of his laugh. She loved *him*.

Wait. *What?*

She looked at him in shock, but fortunately he was still looking at the ceiling as he laughed. Oh, God. She was in love with Blake Randall. The man who abandoned his nephew. The man threatening to build a casino on Gallant Lake. The guy who didn't believe in love. The man who captured her body last night, and now her heart. Was there any chance for this to end well?

"Okay, I confess I didn't *cook* breakfast, but at least I made sure he ate." He noticed her distraction. "Amanda? What's wrong?" She forced herself to smile at him as she shrugged.

He moved to the edge of the bed, cupping her chin in his hand and leaning close to her face. "No regrets. Okay?" He dropped a kiss on her lips. "We'll figure this out."

Her body began to sing as a pulse of energy shot through her. She looked into his eyes. Those eyes that held her safely last night. Those eyes she trusted.

He studied her face. "If you keep looking at me like that, you'll never get out of this bed. And right now I have to go talk to someone in town about some land I'm interested in. I'll be back later. Are you okay?"

Land? The casino. *Damn it.*

"Still working on the casino plan?"

He stopped her with another kiss. "No, sweetheart. This place has become hallowed ground to me. No one's building anything here. No one." A shadow crossed his face for just a moment, then he grinned again. It was a sweet, child-like grin that charmed her completely. "You've ruined my good business sense, girl. Gallant Lake Resort stays whole. Halcyon is my home. My nephew's going to public school. And I have a brave, bewitching woman in my bed."

No casino. Zach in public school. Her in his bed. She threw her arms around his neck and kissed him. He groaned and turned, pressing her back against the bed, returning the kiss. He bit her lower lip and rested his forehead on hers. "I'm not kidding, Amanda. I'll keep you in bed all day long, and then again all night. We'll starve, but we'll die happy. Is that what you want?"

"Yes. But not the dying part." She giggled, then sighed into his neck as he hugged her. "You make me happy, Blake Randall. Scary happy." He lifted his head.

"Scary happy. Yeah, I guess that captures it, doesn't it?" He kissed her quickly, then sat up and rose to his feet. "Drink your coffee and get dressed, lazybones. I'll only be gone for an hour or so, and I promised Zach we'd go fishing."

Chapter Sixteen

She didn't join the boys for their fishing trip in the small aluminum boat. Instead, she curled up in one of the Adirondack chairs by the shore with a romance novel she'd borrowed from Julie. It was almost November, but the sun shone bright and warm. She tried in vain to keep her attention on the book in her hands and not on the incredible sex she'd had with Blake last night.

It was more than sex, of course. She was in love with him. Fingers of panic traced a path up her spine.

After an hour or so, the two fishermen returned to the dock, empty-handed but laughing. Blake surprised her by giving her a warm kiss right in front of Zach. Her face burned, but Zach just smiled and looked away. She frowned at Blake in disapproval, and he laughed.

"It's getting chilly out here, Miss Amanda. Why don't you come inside and I'll pour us both some wine?"

Blake and Zach were laughing upstairs when she came into the house, and another piece of her heart fractured. That voice of fear started whispering again. How long could their little fantasy family life last? Was Blake really ready for a home and a family? Could life here at Halcyon satisfy him for more than a few weeks? He still had an international business empire to run, so he'd have to travel a lot, leaving them behind.

She wanted to believe it could work. Because she was completely and utterly in love with the man. There was no sense in denying it. She just had to figure out exactly what that meant for her heart. And for her future. He walked up behind her as she stood in the living room staring out at the lake. He wrapped one arm around her stomach and pulled her back against him, sliding a glass of wine into her hand as he kissed the top of her head.

"You're thinking too much again."

How did he always know? He squeezed her and answered her unspoken question.

"It's in your shoulders, in your face, in your silence."

"I'm just wondering if we're kidding ourselves here." She hadn't really intended to speak her fears out loud. But there it was. He turned her in his arms.

"Kidding ourselves in what way?"

She sighed and blinked away. "It's like we've been living in a bubble. What will happen to Zach if something happens between us, Blake?"

"Happens, how?"

"We're giving him the illusion that we've become this instant family, and he'll be crushed if that falls apart." She didn't mention that she'd be crushed, too. "He's already been through so much. Are we doing the right thing for him? I mean, it's all fun and games while we sit here in Gallant Lake, but you'll be leaving again, and how appealing is this place going to be to you when the snow starts to fly and you're walking the beaches in Barbados or wherever?"

"What are you talking about?" He stepped back. "What have I done that makes you think I haven't been honest with you?"

She couldn't think of one thing. "Nothing."

"Then what the hell, Amanda?"

"Look, I know how you were raised. I know how driven you are. I know what you think about romance. Are you saying you've become a totally different person in the past few weeks?"

"Yes."

She gasped at how quickly he answered.

His eyes were steady as he held her gaze.

"Yes. I've changed. Haven't you?"

She looked down and thought for a moment. After all, she'd trusted him with her body, when she hadn't been able to do that with any man.

"Yes. I guess I have. But maybe we should take a step back." When would she stop living in fear? Why couldn't she trust him with her heart?

Love is like fool's gold, Amanda. Love is an illusion. A trick. A flicker of a moment that's not worth the resulting trouble.

She slowly opened her eyes the next morning, trying to get her bearings. She turned to look at the source of radiating heat behind her, knowing he was the reason she'd slept so soundly. Good Lord, he was gorgeous.

Blake's face was soft in slumber, but still sexy. His hair fell down over one eye haphazardly, and his lips were curled into an almost-smile, as if he'd just sighed in contentment. The sheets were down around his waist, so she got to peruse his broad chest, covered with dark curls. She couldn't help reaching out to trace her fingers down his sternum. His eyes snapped open when she touched him, and they were smoldering.

He reached his hand out and rested it on her cheek, giving her a crooked, sleepy grin. She immediately decided this was her favorite look on him. Rumpled, half-awake, aroused and in lo—

No! She gave herself a hard mental shake. He was not in love with her, regardless of her feelings for him. He was the guy who didn't believe in love. Didn't have time for it. Thought it was foolish. He could easily betray her, just like all the other men in her life had done. Frowning at her troubled expression, he stroked her bottom lip lightly with his thumb. He leaned in for a deep kiss, and she forgot what she was worrying about. He pulled her under his body without breaking contact with her lips. He traced kisses lightly down her neck and lifted the hem of her nightgown. He left her only long enough to get a condom from the nightstand, but even that was too long. She whispered his name.

"I'm here. I'm here, beautiful. I'll always be here…"

She decided to believe him a while longer and lost herself to the sensation of him filling her completely. She arched into him and closed her eyes, focusing only on the wonder of Blake making soft, sweet love to her. Her pulse began to race. She whispered his name over and over, and he growled as he became more aggressive. She wasn't afraid. In fact, she was eager. She dug her nails into his back and cried his name one last time as her body fell apart. He joined her wordlessly, groaning as he fell onto her, breathing hard.

Finally he spoke. "Best. Alarm clock. Ever."

She giggled into his ear. "Speaking of alarm clocks, Zach will be up soon, and if he comes looking for me…"

"How can you talk about *Zach* after we just set the sheets on fire? Let me just enjoy the moment, will you?" He chuckled and bit her lightly on the shoulder. "Besides, I can't move right now, even if the entire village of Gallant Lake came into this room. Even if Madeleine Pendleton herself joined us. I'm not moving."

She tightened her arms around him. He might break her heart someday. But until then, he was hers. He moved his weight off her and pulled her close. She nuzzled his chest and kissed him there.

"Just stay with me a few more minutes," he sighed. "Let me hold you." His breathing changed, and she knew he'd fallen asleep. She snuggled into him, but if she closed her eyes she'd never get Zach off to school. And she certainly didn't want him to walk in and catch them together in bed. She slid carefully out from under the covers and left Blake sleeping there.

He didn't come downstairs until after Zach left. She couldn't stop the laughter that bubbled up when he walked into the kitchen, looking so very pleased with himself.

"And here we go with the laughter after sex again." He held his hands to his chest in mock offense. "I'm going to get a complex."

"Sorry." She slid a mug of coffee across the island to him. "You just look so totally... I don't know...satisfied? Like a Cheshire cat."

"Satisfied is definitely how I'm feeling this morning. I didn't even feel you leave the bed. Is Zach off to school?"

"Of course. You're the only lazybones this morning." She reached for the paper bag on the counter, knowing Blake liked a simple breakfast. "Bagel?"

He nodded and she split the bagel and dropped it into the toaster. Her phone started ringing in her back pocket.

She did a little victory dance when the call ended, then had to explain it when she saw Blake's surprise.

"Your desk is ready! There's a guy in town who builds furniture, and I talked him into refinishing that antique desk I found in the attic." The heavily carved mahogany desk had been buried under boxes and drop cloths when she'd gone exploring up there. As soon as she uncovered it, she knew it would be perfect for Blake's office. "This project is almost done!"

Was it just her, or had an awkward silence fallen like a giant wet blanket over the kitchen? Blake shrugged, ate the last of his bagel and grabbed his travel mug of coffee. "Sounds great, babe."

So apparently it *was* just Amanda who felt the end racing at them. At her. He started to walk past, then stopped and gave her a fierce hug and kiss.

"Relax. The house is wrapping up, but you and I are nowhere *near* done. I told you I want your help with the resorts, and I've got plans, baby."

The corner of Blake's mouth tipped up into a crooked grin. "I need to go make some calls, but let's go into town for pizza when Zach gets home. We'll have a family night, okay?"

The words were right there on her lips when he kissed her and walked away. She *wanted* to tell him how much she loved him. Soon.

Blake's best friend let out a long, low whistle on the other end of the phone.

"Let me get this straight—your interior designer pretended to be someone else to get the job. And instead of firing her, you're…dating?"

Blake didn't answer. Amanda was walking down to the lakeshore with a warm sweater draped over her shoulders. He'd lost track of the conversation when she stopped to look back at the house. He doubted she could see him standing at the living room windows, but her shoulders straightened nonetheless. Halcyon was working its magic on her once again. He couldn't claim to understand it, but he knew she got strength from this pink castle.

"Blake? You still with me?"

Andy McCormack's voice interrupted his thoughts. "Yeah, man. Sorry. I was watching my girl walking outside."

"She must be something pretty special to pierce *your* armor."

"She's tough, Andy. Strong. Beautiful."

Andy laughed. "Oh, man, you're a goner!"

They'd been best friends since meeting at Harvard and were investors in each other's companies. Andy's company, McCormack Security, provided bodyguards, security systems and planning to companies and celebrities all over the world. Jamal had worked for Andy before coming to head up security at Gallant Lake.

Blake settled back in his chair. Amanda was walking along the shore now. She bent to pick up a stone, sending it skipping across the smooth surface of the lake.

"Okay, clearly you're not ready to talk about your new girl. What did the preservation society say when you told them you scrapped the casino plans? Have things calmed down any?"

The episodes of vandalism were ticking up in frequency and intensity, although the official members of the group claimed they had nothing to do with it.

"I haven't told them yet. I have some investors that aren't too happy about it, so I want to be sure I smooth those feathers before it goes public. And I need to have answers for the locals who *wanted* those jobs. I'll have to convince them we can create new jobs by renovating the resort and getting businesses to improve downtown Gallant Lake to draw in more people."

"And your family? What are they going to say when you bring her to Christmas dinner?"

Blake scoffed. "As if I'd sit down for Christmas dinner with any of them. They were never officially part of the casino. Father wanted too big a piece of the pie, so we never signed a deal. I'm not sure Nathan knows that, though." His brother seemed to assume the casino was a family project, if only because it was located in New York. But *assuming* was never a good business practice. Blake didn't want to discuss his family, though, and he knew the one topic Andy was always ready to talk about these days— his new fiancée.

"You still planning a Barbados wedding? Speaking of which, when do I get to meet the woman crazy enough to agree to marry you?" His friend met a feisty Southern girl while on vacation a few months ago, and Andy fell like a ton of bricks. He'd popped the question before Blake had a chance to meet her.

"Barbados next spring. Caroline's coming to the Builders Ball in New York. Are you bringing Amanda?"

Damn. He hadn't even thought about the annual must-attend event for every real estate investor on the East Coast. Would Amanda want to be in that coldhearted pack of over-achieving snobs? Would it trigger a panic attack?

"I'm not sure." He cleared his throat and changed the subject again. "I still can't believe you're getting married, Andy."

"Believe it, my friend. I've never been happier. And it seems to me like you've got it pretty bad for this Amanda woman."

Blake shook his head. Yeah, he had it bad, all right. But marriage? It was way too soon to be going there, even if Andy and Caroline had gotten engaged barely six weeks after meeting. He ignored the comment and finished up the conversation. He wasn't ready to discuss his feelings for Amanda yet. Not even with his best friend. Not until he'd sorted them out for himself.

Blake leaned against the doorway to the living room the following Sunday evening and smiled. Amanda and Zachary were on the sofa together, watching a very loud movie about cars that transformed into alien robots. There was a bowl of popcorn between them, and they were giggling as they snuggled under a soft wool blanket.

Andy was right—Amanda had pierced his well-worn armor somehow. Torn down his carefully built wall. Thoroughly trashed his No Surprises Lifestyle. His goals had swung sharply from business success at all costs to keeping her happy and safe every day of her life.

And she'd done it without even breaking a sweat. First she agitated him to his breaking point and beyond, then she reeled him in for the kill with her brutal honesty and wisdom. He was in awe of her. She'd trusted her body to him in spite of her past, in spite of her fears. And now he wanted nothing more than to be with her every moment. He'd protect her with everything he had.

His stomach twisted. Relationships had always been a losing proposition for him. They were never worth the energy invested. Sure, people tossed around the *L* word like it meant something, but he'd learned differently time and time again. Why even pretend it was real? Look at the disastrous track record his family had in relationships. It was like they were cursed.

That old argument, the one he'd been clinging to for so long, suddenly sounded hollow. It was different with Amanda. There was a glimmer of something inside of him that had simply never existed until she came waltzing into his house. Was it hope?

Zach threw a piece of popcorn at Amanda and she caught it in her mouth, making the boy laugh. Tiffany's little boy. Zachary was Blake's chance to do things right. To make up for the way he let his sister down. His parents should have loved her better, damn it. If no one else, *they* should have loved their beautiful baby girl. He'd tried to love her enough for everyone, but he couldn't do it. It was too late for him to save Tiffany, but it wasn't too late for Zach. The kid had his mother's sense of humor. Her laugh. Her heart. He'd taken care of Amanda while Blake was halfway around the world being a jackass.

Warmth blossomed inside of him, as if he could actually feel his heart growing. He thought of that Christmas cartoon character whose heart grew so much with love that it burst right out of his chest. Yeah, this woman had done something to him, all right. It was a mind-boggling turn of events. He'd teased her earlier about remodeling him along with the house, and in truth, she'd done just that.

She looked up and saw him standing there, then smiled and tilted her head questioningly. He pushed away from the wall and walked over, sitting on the floor in front of her and Zach. He handed her one of the wineglasses he'd been carrying. She massaged the top of his head absently with her fingertips as the good robots started defeating the bad robots on screen. He leaned his head back against her knee and sighed.

This is what love felt like. He was in love with her. He was in love with the woman who challenged him and changed him and made him whole. He was in love with Amanda Lowery.

He was standing at the edge of a cliff, and the drop was shrouded in fog. Would he fly if he stepped off? Would he crash to the earth? It didn't matter. His heart had already leaped, so he was going to have to follow. Life as he'd known it was over. And he was okay with that.

Chapter Seventeen

Blake was later than usual getting to the office the next morning, and he was feeling pretty damned good about it. He was late because Amanda insisted he drive Zach to school. She insisted because Zach missed the bus. Zach missed the bus because they all overslept. They overslept because he'd woken Amanda sometime before dawn with a kiss in a place she'd never been kissed before. Yeah— totally worth being late. Over the past few days, he'd discovered sharing a bed with Amanda was worth pretty much anything.

Her sharp intake of breath when she'd woken had been quickly replaced with soft moans of pleasure while he'd explored every inch of her. The sun had been just beginning to rise when they'd finally dozed off in a tangle of arms and legs. By the time they'd woken again, there'd been no way Zach was catching the bus. She'd pretended to be upset, but he was pretty sure that was more embarrassment than anything else; as if a ten-year-old was going to guess what made Uncle Blake and Miss Amanda so very sleepy and smiley.

A soft knock at his office door brought him back to the here and now. He waved Julie in.

"Mr. Randall…"

"Julie, you're one of Amanda's closest friends. I think you can call me 'Blake' and still maintain our professional relationship during working hours."

Her brows lifted in surprise.

"I think so, too, Blake. Thank you. I just wanted to remind

you about the conference call. I've got it set up on your line, and the Miami management staff is standing by."

"Hmm? Oh, of course. I almost forgot." He was the one who'd scheduled the call to discuss the upcoming celebrity wedding in Miami. Even after the call started, he couldn't stop thinking about how Amanda looked in the moonlight last night, golden hair flamed out against the pillows as she whispered his name.

When he heard a sharp knock on his closed office door a few hours later, he figured it was Julie again. He couldn't have been more surprised, or more disappointed, at who opened the door when he called out.

His father and brother walked in without bothering to greet him. Nathan's eyes narrowed as he looked around the large office, taking in every custom detail as well as the panoramic view of Gallant Lake and the mountains beyond it through the windows that lined one wall. There was a reason Nathan had never been invited to the resort, and this was it. For all of his own personal wealth, Nathan was openly jealous of Blake's self-made success. Blake had broken free of their father's influence, and Nathan never had the backbone to do the same. Their father glanced around the room dismissively, clearly unimpressed.

Blake felt a sharp pain in his temple at the sight of his so-called family standing in his private office. The headache prompted a blunt question.

"What the hell are you two doing here?"

He didn't doubt for a minute that they were here to make trouble. His father took one of the small chairs in front of Blake's desk. Nathan stood by the windows, hands in his pockets, and barely acknowledged Blake's presence. But he gave away his weakness when his eyes kept darting to their father for validation. It was sad, really.

He might be five years older than Blake, but Nathan was clueless if he thought he was ever going to win respect from their father. First, Edwin Randall's respect was meaningless, because the man was clueless. Second, he was too self-absorbed to acknowledge anyone else's accomplishments, even those of his own sons.

"Father. Nathan." Blake nodded in their general direction. "Let me rephrase in case you didn't understand the first time. Kindly explain your presence on my property."

His father harrumphed. "We're here to discuss the casino. You brought this investment proposal to us, and I'm not liking the rumors I'm hearing. This type of gamesmanship is beneath us all, son."

Blake just shook his head. "It was a proposal. Not a done deal. No signatures."

Nathan finally joined the conversation, taking a seat next to their father.

"Rumor has it you're backing out of the casino plans, even though you nearly have the votes you need in Albany. We did our homework after you brought the idea to us. If you're really out, then we're in. We want to buy the resort, but if you won't sell, we're prepared to build a casino elsewhere in town."

Randall men rarely laughed, which was probably why Nathan and his father looked so stunned when Blake started to. Loudly. And for a good long time.

His father sputtered for a minute, then stood, trying and failing to appear patriarchal. "If the rumors are just a smoke screen and you're still planning on building the casino, you'd better plan on having us as partners, son. If not, we'll build our own."

Blake stopped chuckling and rose to his feet. They stared hard into each other's eyes until his father's gaze finally broke away in defeat.

"Good luck with that, gentlemen."

Nathan jumped to his feet, placing his hands on Blake's

desk and leaning forward with a scowl. He was doing his best to look and sound menacing.

"You can't stop us. The community wants the jobs. You'll cut us in, or we'll just set up shop on the other side of town."

"Really?" Blake casually stacked some papers on his desk, as if he was bored with the conversation. "I happen to know who owns the land on the other side of town, and he's not interested in selling."

Father looked confused, but Nathan's thin smile showed no signs of surprise.

"So it's true. *You're* the one buying up all the property around here. You think you're so clever, convincing everyone you're the guy in the white hat. Setting up house in that ostentatious castle. Sending Zachary to the local school. Screwing your designer."

Blake's pretense of nonchalance ended at those final three words. His hands curled into fists, crumpling paper as they did. Nathan blanched, but kept talking.

"Yes, we know all about your little girlfriend. Did you know Amanda Lowery lost her last job because there were rumors she was committing fraud? She was unemployed and nearly homeless when she set her hooks into you. And you want that gold digger raising Zachary?" Nathan's confidence was building again, his smile thin and threatening. "I wonder what a family court judge would think of your choices for Zachary? Maybe Michaela and I should seek custody, just to protect the poor boy. Think about that before you make any decisions about Gallant Lake, little brother."

Blake met Nathan's pale-eyed stare without blinking. His body might be frozen in place, but in his mind, he was pounding his brother's face into a bloody pulp. And maybe someday he'd do just that. But not today. It would be a show of weakness, and he wouldn't give them the pleasure. He could deal with Nathan and Michaela. They were serpents with teeth, but without venom.

"Stay away from my family, Nathan. You and Father both. Get the hell out of my resort. Stay the hell out of Gallant Lake, and stop wasting your breath on empty threats." He leaned forward and felt a jolt of satisfaction when Nathan backed away. "Don't you ever so much as *speak* Amanda's or Tiffany's names in front of me again. You've never been fit to lick the dirt off the bottom of their shoes."

He walked out of his own office, ignoring his brother's shouted vows to destroy him.

There was only one person capable of doing that, and she was sitting in a pink castle at the top of the hill.

Amanda was full of restless energy after breakfast. The workers were pounding away in the office, and that crew always made her uptight. Sure enough, there was Russ hunched over the table saw by the windows, as if he was trying to make his large form look smaller. As usual, he glanced up at her and glowered when he made eye contact. He always seemed so angry. He'd been friends with the guy Bobby fired for ranting about the casino, so it made sense that he was just as opposed to it and the Randall family. But he didn't seem to mind taking their money. She walked out into the main hall, telling herself she was being paranoid.

Maybe it was the conversation she'd had with Zach's teacher yesterday. She'd gone in for a conference, and noticed some anti-casino pamphlets on the corner of his desk. Thinking of Blake's promise that the resort would stay as is, she'd told Bruce he didn't need to print any more flyers or signs. She'd told him she'd heard a very reliable rumor that the casino plans were dead. But Bruce had been skeptical.

"No offense, Amanda," he'd said, "but it's hard to believe that when Blake Randall is still buying up property all over the county. I don't think he can be trusted. He just closed on the Maguire farm last week."

She hadn't argued, since Blake said the news of the casino being stopped wasn't official yet. There could be a dozen reasons why he'd be buying property, if he even *was*. It wouldn't be the first time some wild rumor about him had been spread around town. But she couldn't shake the conversation.

She had no reason in the world to be so edgy after the way Blake had woken her in the wee hours of the morning. Good Lord, what that man could do with his mouth! She blushed, even though no one was around. Sizzling sex was no excuse for sleeping that late. Or maybe it was. She ran her fingers back and forth on the mantel, lost in thoughts of what she might do to him tonight to return the favor…

"Oh, my God!" Julie laughed as she walked into the room. "I want some of what you've been having. You look positively dreamy eyed. Am I too late for lunch?"

Amanda cringed at being caught in a sexy daydream.

"Hi, Jules, I didn't hear you come in."

"Sorry if I startled you, but one of Bobby's guys left the door open. We're still on, right?"

"Yes, of course. I've got lunch set up in the solarium."

"Do I even need to guess who's got you so distracted this morning?" Julie grinned as she sat down and took a sandwich from the platter. "And just so you know, Blake's sporting a very similar postcoital glow."

"Julie!" She couldn't help but laugh. "Be quiet! I don't want the workers hearing about my coital *anything*. God, I can't believe I'm so transparent."

"Honey, you and I are friends. Of course I notice when you get all dewy-eyed and glowy. Things are getting serious?"

A familiar panic climbed her spine. Were *they* getting serious? Or was it just *her*? She took a few bites of her sandwich while her mind tried to make sense of things. She and Blake were sleeping together, living together, raising Zach together, but…so far he'd only talked about her *working* for him in the future. Nothing about what their relationship might be.

"I don't know, Julie. I'm so confused right now. It's not easy for me to trust anyone, even Blake, with my heart. I hate it, but my mind is always looking for what's going to go wrong, no matter how good things are." She took a sip of tea. "Christmas is less than two months away, and I don't know what his plans are. Will I still be here?"

Julie laughed. "My guess is a solid yes to that question. He's nuts for you. He asked me to confirm two tickets for the Builders Ball gala in Manhattan this weekend, and I'm *sure* he's planning on taking you."

It was the first she'd heard of anything called a "Builders Ball" *or* plans for the weekend. Amanda thought about what Bruce said. "Do you know anything about Blake buying land for the casino?"

Julie's eyes went wide. "That was an unexpected change of subject. I know he's met with some Realtors, but I got the impression he was backing off on the casino plans. Why?"

She told Julie about her conversation with Bruce Hoffman. She told her what Blake said about not changing the resort. But he never actually said he wasn't building a casino *somewhere*.

A rough laugh startled both women. Russ was standing at the entrance to the solarium, a smirk on his unshaven face. His clothes were rumpled, as usual, and Amanda could smell the stale scent of cigarette smoke from where she was sitting. He spoke before she could question why he was there.

"You still don't get it, do you? Randall's out to own the whole town. The whole damned *county*. He's snapping up everything that goes on the market. Pretty soon there won't be anyone left to fight him on that damned casino." He gave her a malevolent glare. "Unless someone stops him."

"Russ!" Bobby came up behind him. "What the hell are you doing in here? I told you to work on the trim in the office, which is that way. Don't let me catch you bothering anyone again."

Russ held his hands up, mumbled an apology and walked away. Bobby looked at the two women.

"What was he saying to you? The guy's worked with me before, but his attitude lately sucks. I can tell him to go…"

Amanda shook her head.

"You're almost done here, Bobby, and you need all hands on deck. It's fine." She gave him a smile. "But thanks for watching out for us."

Amanda and Julie stared at each other over the table after Bobby left. Blake said Gallant Lake was hallowed ground. Was he only talking about the resort?

"Julie, do you think he'd build a casino somewhere else in town and claim he'd kept his word?"

Julie ran her fingers up and down the handle of her teacup, frowning. "I *want* to say no. And I really can't believe he'd do that. But…" She looked over to Amanda. "His father and brother came to the resort today to meet with Blake. They were just going in when I left. They didn't look very happy, but…"

Blake never had anything good to say about his father and brother, but they *were* real estate developers. And they were family.

"Bruce and Russ both said he's buying land…"

"Well, we can check that." Julie sat back in her chair. "I help Bobby with his building permits, so I know my way around the county's website. I can pull the tax records online. If Blake's buying land, we'll know it, but I'm sure it's all just a crazy rumor."

She might be right, but it was a rumor that tapped into

Amanda's greatest fear—that everything in Gallant Lake was an illusion. That Blake couldn't be trusted. That he could betray her the same way all the other men in her life had done. Her stepfather. Jimmy Waldron. David Franklin. The creep who attacked her in New York.

There was a drumbeat hammering in her heart, warning her to think before reacting. That Blake *wasn't* like the others. That she didn't know everything. That she was jumping to conclusions. That she had no right to judge.

"Amanda? Tell me what you're thinking."

She looked up at the ceiling and blinked away tears. "I know I'm too quick to believe the worst, but I'm terrified that loving Blake gives him the power to really hurt me. That might just be a hurt I can't recover from." She met Julie's worried look. "I *am* in love with him."

"That's pretty easy to see. I think he's falling in love with you, too. The way he looks at you gives me goose bumps. He's been a different man since you arrived."

Was it possible he felt the same way she did? A flush of heat swept from her toes to her scalp as her heart whispered, *I told you so*. She took a deep breath and noticed the light fragrance of roses in the room. One of the random things she'd always blamed on Madeleine, but there had to be a logical reason the room always smelled like flowers. She stood, then answered Julie's questioning gaze.

"I'm going to grab my laptop. I'll be right back."

"Are you sure you want to do this?" Julie hedged.

Amanda closed her eyes in resignation. "I need to know."

Chapter Eighteen

Twenty pages of tax property records were stacked on the round table in front of Amanda. She'd printed the property records after Julie found them all. Blake's name was on every one of them.

"Hey." Blake's deep voice made her jump. He was standing just inside the solarium, rubbing the back of his neck absently. Lines of tension radiated from the corners of his eyes. He looked as on edge as she felt.

She stood slowly, her heart racing. She wanted to run into his arms. She frowned. She had to be strong enough to do what she *needed* to do, not what she *wanted* to do. She had to protect her heart. She rested her hands on the tax papers.

"Are you building a casino here?"

He rolled his eyes. "Not you, too. Why would you even ask me that question after I told you I wasn't?"

"Why won't you *answer*? You're buying land all over town, Blake. And outside of town, all over the county. Twenty different properties." She held up the papers and shook them. "Why do that if you aren't building the casino?"

He stepped forward, his mouth falling open.

"You pulled tax records on me? You've gathered the evidence and convicted me before you even asked a single question. What the hell, Amanda?"

He's right. He's right. He's right.

Her heart hammered out the mantra, but she was too determined to turn back now. She had to be sure. She had to have answers, no matter how much it hurt. "You still haven't answered my question."

He was standing across the table from her now, and she watched a parade of emotions cross his face. Hurt. Fury. Sadness. That drumbeat in her heart grew louder, begging her to stop.

"No, I'm *not* building a casino—here or anywhere. But I've told you that already, haven't I?"

"Then why are you buying up every parcel of land that's available? Houses. Farms. Businesses. Acreage. Why?"

His fingers curled tightly, then slowly released, as if he was trying to curb his anger. He muttered something to himself, then took a deep breath and met her eyes.

"It's not what it looks like." He gestured to the papers now scattered across the table where she'd dropped them.

"It's not what it looks like…" she echoed.

Slow down. Slow down. Slow down…

It was too late to stop the words she was thinking from spilling out. "In my experience, when a man says that, it's usually *exactly* what it looks like."

His shoulders dropped. "Damn it, Amanda, have I ever given you a reason to doubt me? Do you really think I'm anything like Franklin or whomever else from your past you think I'm channeling? This is *me*."

She wanted to believe him, but fear whispered to her from the edges of the darkness closing in on her. She turned away and moved to the window.

"Were your father and brother here because of the casino?"

"Yes, but not…"

She faced him again, unable to stop the question before blurting it out. "Are you going into the city this weekend? Alone?"

Because he certainly hadn't invited *her*. Blake's eyes closed slowly, and she could almost see him counting to himself, trying to control his reaction. After a long, tense pause, he opened those eyes just as slowly.

"If you're going to turn into a jealous mistress every time someone—"

"A mistress? Did you just call me a *mistress*?"

"You know that's not what I meant."

"Do I?"

He stared at her a long moment, then sighed. "Well, if you don't, then what the hell are we doing together?"

Her heart wanted this to stop. *She* wanted to stop. She wanted to stop hurting him. She wanted to stop destroying whatever they'd been building together at Halcyon. But she was no good at this. No good at trusting.

"So tell me about this Builders Ball. Who are you planning to take?"

Blake leaned forward and slammed his hands down on the table with so much force the property records went flying in different directions. They fluttered down to the tile floor like the dead leaves falling off the autumn trees outside.

"Are you kidding me? I was going to take *you*, but that feels like a really bad idea right now. In fact, the only thing that feels like a good idea is me getting the hell out of here so we don't do any more damage than we already have."

She knew it. He was always going to leave her. Her terror made her next words come out in an angry hiss.

"Well, don't let me stop you. Go ahead and leave! Go plan your big casino and all those wonderful jobs you talked about. Go back to your real life and your fancy balls and all your traveling. You were never going to stay here anyway, were you?"

He spread his arms wide in an angry gesture.

"Now you're just looking for ways to keep this ridiculous argument going. This is the kind of bullshit I hate. The stupid games. The petty jealousy. The verbal traps.

I get enough of this crap from my family, and I sure as hell don't need it from you."

He turned away, then spun back again, as if he was having the same kind of internal battle she was. His shoulders dropped in resignation.

"Amanda, I don't even know what to say to you right now. After last night. After this weekend. After I..." He stopped and his expression hardened. "If you can't trust me, if you think so little of me...if you'll fall for every whispered rumor...then what the hell are we doing here?"

Anger and hurt built in the silence until it shimmered in the air between them.

And still she couldn't stop talking. She had some visceral need to be the one to push them apart, as if she could protect herself that way. As if it wasn't already too late.

"What are we doing? Apparently...nothing."

She watched the shutters close behind his eyes. His emotionless face scared her much more than his anger had.

"I'm going to leave before one of us says something unforgivable. And we're getting pretty goddamned close to that right now." His voice was flat, but his words still felt like knives. "God*damn* relationships. I'll never learn."

He stared at the floor for a long beat, then turned away. The pain in her chest was so intense that her hand rose to cover it. A cloud must have passed over the house, because the light from the windows dimmed, and the room turned sharply colder. When she looked back to the doorway, Blake was gone.

His name escaped her lips in a whisper. She rushed to the door, but by the time she reached the front steps, his black SUV was already spinning its tires on the way down the driveway.

Chapter Nineteen

Every passing hour made Amanda feel worse. It was Thursday afternoon, and Blake hadn't called or texted since he left in a cloud of dust on Monday, although he did talk to Zach every day. She knew he was in New York because Zach told her as much, but she didn't know when, or even *if*, he was coming back to Halcyon. And it was all her fault.

Julie kept offering to stop by, but Amanda needed to be alone. She wanted to wallow in her pain and she didn't want anyone trying to talk her out of it. She deserved this. She paced the house endlessly, trying to understand what had happened. What she'd done. Why she'd done it. Whether or not she'd been right. And whether or not it could be fixed.

As usual, she ended up in Blake's office. The room was almost done. A dark Persian rug covered the hardwood floors. One long wall was lined with mahogany bookcases stretching to the high ceiling. An old-fashioned library ladder on wheels would be the final touch, giving access to the highest shelves. They just needed to finish the trim work and install the rail the ladder would slide on, and the room would be complete.

The desk had been delivered yesterday. The antique from Halcyon's attic still held a few secrets. The refinisher found several hidden compartments and false drawer bottoms. Most opened easily with spring mechanisms, but there was one, in the back of the lower drawer, that was locked up tight. A filigreed lock showed where a tiny key would fit. Everyone agreed it would be a shame to risk destroying something so delicately made. For now, it would remain sealed.

She ran her fingers over the carved edges of the desk, wishing it was Blake she was touching. With a sigh, she set her phone on the speaker dock on the corner of the desk and started her newest playlist—a repeating cycle of heartbreak.

The curtains swayed behind her as if someone walked past them. Maybe Halcyon's lovesick ghost was nearby.

"Madeleine, you're wasting your time with Blake and me. It's hopeless."

"Miss Amanda? Who are you talking to? Is Uncle Blake on the phone?"

Zachary stood in the doorway, head tipped to the side, looking at her strangely.

"Um...no. No one's on the phone. I was just talking to myself. I do that sometimes. Pretty silly, huh?"

He nodded, but didn't seem convinced. "When is Uncle Blake coming home? Why is he staying in New York this week?"

She wanted to scream to the rafters that *she* was the reason Blake wasn't with them. That she had hurt him and pushed him away, and she didn't know when he might be back. But instead, she smiled warmly and tried to reassure a young boy who had no idea that the two adults in his life had made such a monumental mess of things.

"I hope he'll be home next week. He has something to do in the city this weekend." She tried to distract Zach. "Are the boys coming over to swim today?"

Zach's new friends at school had enjoyed the indoor pool at the resort several times in the past few weeks. He was still enrolled in the Gallant Lake Elementary School as Zachary Lowery, but his closest friends now knew his real name, and that he actually lived in the castle on the hill. They were enjoying the perks of being friends with the resort owner's nephew.

"We're not swimming today. Maybe tomorrow." He shrugged, still staring at her curiously. "Did you and Uncle Blake have a fight?"

This boy was depending on them and saw them as a couple. As a family. *His* family. He deserved better than to worry about the adults in his life arguing on a regular basis.

"We had a…disagreement, Zach. Nothing for you to worry about." She hoped that was true.

"I heard you yelling the other day about all the places Uncle Blake is buying. Why did that make you so mad?"

Amanda gestured to the chair in front of the desk. "Have a seat, Zach." He sat in the chair and waited, with that wise-beyond-his-years expression she loved so much. She loved this boy. She loved his uncle.

"Your uncle and I are having a disagreement about something he wants to build here in Gallant Lake."

"The gambling place?"

She wasn't surprised he'd heard about it, probably in school.

"Yes, the casino."

"But he doesn't want to build it anymore. He told me so."

A pulse of hope made her sit straighter, followed quickly by a jolt of panic. Had she been wrong about everything? "When did he tell you that, Zach?"

"When we were fishing. He said he used to want to build a big place that would give lots of people jobs—" Amanda started to roll her eyes, but Zach kept talking "—but he decided it was more important to…pre…present…pres…"

"Preserve?" she prompted him, feeling her heart start to pick up speed.

"Yeah! He said he wants to preserve Gallant Lake. He said he was going to keep Gallant Lake safe from Uncle Nathan and Grandfather."

Maybe Zach had misunderstood his uncle. If not, she'd

chased Blake away over nothing. "Are you sure he didn't say he wanted to protect the *casino* from them?"

He gave her that exasperated look only a child can give an adult and get away with, as if she'd just said the stupidest thing. Then he shook his head.

"No, Miss Amanda. He said he's buying up everything for sale so Uncle Nathan and Grandfather *can't* buy it. He said they can't build anything without land. He said it was costing him a bunch of money, but it was worth it to keep Halcyon safe for his family. For you and me."

"Me and you?" The words were barely a whisper. Family. They were a family. Blake had been fighting to protect them, and she'd rewarded him by throwing accusations at him.

"Yeah." There was that condescending look again. "He said this is our home now—you, me and him. And he told me a man's job is to keep his home safe for the people he loves."

Her racing heart skidded to a stop. Blake wasn't buying land for the reason she'd accused him of. He was buying it to protect Gallant Lake. She'd been such a fool.

For the people he loves...

"Miss Amanda, are you okay?"

She blinked back fresh tears and did her best to reassure Zach. "Yes, honey. I think I just might be. Come here and give me a hug, then go do your homework, okay?"

He groaned, but did as she asked, running out of the room and leaping to slap his hand against the top of the doorway with boyish enthusiasm. She leaned back in the chair in stunned silence for a very long time, trying to absorb what Zach had just told her. She couldn't stop thinking about what Blake had done, and how she'd repaid him by jumping to conclusions and refusing to trust him.

Her heart beat out a steady tattoo of *I told you so. I told you so. I told you so.*

He'd left her. She'd accused him of lying, and all along he'd been trying to build a safe home for them here. He'd never once given her a reason to doubt him, but she just couldn't help herself. She dropped her head into her hands and wept at the damage her fear had created.

The evening passed in a fog. If Zach noticed her distraction at dinner, he didn't let on. He talked about school and his friends and wanting to learn how to play golf and wondering if his uncle would teach him. They watched a movie together after dinner, then she sent him up to bed. She found herself back in Blake's office, pacing the floor, trying to figure out how she could fix this. She was drawn to the enormous desk again, as if it might hold a secret answer for her.

She pulled out the lower right drawer, staring at the locked compartment. Elaborate brass filigree surrounded the tiny round hole for a key. The filigree looked familiar, and she knelt to get a closer look. As her fingers traced the unusual design of interlocking circles, she remembered where she'd seen that design before. She sat back on her heels.

It was *impossible*. It had to be impossible. Talking to a ghost she laughingly *chose* to believe in was one thing, but to think everything was set in motion back in August when she bought an antique evening purse…it was impossible. She ran up the staircase to the yellow bedroom. The delicate beaded purse she'd bought in Gallant Lake in August was sitting in the closet, wrapped in tissue paper. She unsnapped it and reached inside, pulling out a tiny key with a filigree top that matched the design around the lock in the desk exactly.

The key to Otis's desk.

In Madeleine's purse.

Back down in the office, she wasn't at all surprised when

the tiny key slid into the lock perfectly. There was a barely perceptible click when she turned it, and the front of the compartment fell forward.

The grayed papers inside looked fragile, and she reached for them gingerly. It was a stack of letters, tied together with a pale blue ribbon. Each letter was tucked carefully into an envelope, addressed to Otis Pendleton in Manhattan. These were Madeleine's letters to her husband, carefully protected all these years. Amanda removed them from the drawer and noticed a familiar scent. She lifted them to her face. Roses. Madeleine had sprinkled her letters with rosewater.

She untied the ribbon and spread the letters across the desk. They spanned nearly three decades, from the beginning of the Pendletons' marriage to the very end of it. It felt voyeuristic to read these intimate letters from a hundred years ago, but there was no way she could resist. "Here we go, Madeleine. Let's see what you have to say."

Amanda read for endless hours, eventually moving to an easy chair close to the fire with a glass of wine. The letters were sweetly written in the language of another time. The depth of love in Madeleine's words made her heart ache.

September 18, 1903

My darling Otis,
There are weeks when I curse this arrangement we have made ourselves prisoner to. I adore this insane pink palace you built for me, but to live here alone for days on end is torture of the highest degree. You, my dearest love, are in the noisy metropolis alone (how I pray that you are alone!). Yes, you will tell me 'tis foolish to fret like this, but as the nights grow longer and colder, I spend more time walking the halls of Halcyon with Doubt as my only companion.

I worry that you'll forget me, and that some other woman might just capture the heart and body I claim as mine...

October 27, 1903

Oh, Sweetest One,
You were right to scold me so fiercely last weekend. That dark disease of jealousy drove me nearly mad. I would never betray you—I'd rather die. I know I will be true as surely as I know that I am breathing. So how could I believe that your love is somehow less than mine? How could I insult you in that manner? Oh, how I hated to hear those words from your lips, because their truth seared my heart. Thank you for tolerating my silly fears, and for reassuring me yet again that you love me, and only me...

January 16, 1904

...I believe I had more pleasure from the giving of your Christmas gift than you had in receiving it, my love. The look in your eyes when I told you I was carrying your child is something I will treasure all my life. To think that the passion we share so wantonly in our bedroom has brought forth this blessing! Yes, I blush to think of it, but I am insanely proud of it, as well. It is intoxicating to think that your warm body against mine could produce life. I love you, dearest, and you will be a marvelous father...

July 22, 1917

Sweetest love,
The simmering, sultry days of midsummer are upon

us. I've found these early hours on the balcony to be my favorite time. I like to lean on the warm walls of Halcyon and think long and often useless thoughts. I sit here and pretend that Emily is alive. Our darling fifth and surely final child, taken from us so cruelly. She was so tiny at birth, but how she fought to stay with us. But even the magic of Halcyon could not keep her from God's waiting embrace. I miss her so! Otis, Jr., Andrew, Michael and little Tabitha need us, so survive we must. Yes, I am stricken with grief, but I need to feel your sure hands on my body once again. Come home to me, darling. We can survive whatever life flings in our path, as long as we are together...

June 7, 1929

My darling, I cannot believe that we have now held four weddings here at Halcyon! And wasn't Tabby the most beautiful bride last Sunday? You may have noticed your silly wife could not stop crying throughout the ceremony. I watched her come down those stairs in my own wedding dress, and was swept away to our wedding day so many years ago. You are still the one and only love of my life, Otis, and I am amazed every day at the joy you bring to me. This house is a testimony to that love, and I see you and feel you in every stone. We have built a magical place here, my darling, and we have been happier than surely any mortal deserves...

September 21, 1929

...If only I were there to hold you today, my love. I know it had to be beyond painful to dismiss your own brother, but I say "good riddance" to him. He

*was a horrid business partner and a worse brother.
The crash of the London markets proves you were
right to be concerned over his rash investments. I am
confident you can recover from whatever damage he
has done to the firm with his foolhardy decisions...*

October 25, 1929

*...I know that times are looking desperately dark and
dire, my love. It has been many years since you chose
to stay in the city to work over the weekend instead
of coming home to my waiting arms. I understand,
but it pains me nonetheless. I may just come to the
city and fetch you myself! Regardless of how this all
turns, we have each other, and we have Halcyon. And
frankly, dearest one, even if we lose Halcyon, it will
stand here for someone else. If you and I end our days
in a shanty, I know that a new love story will eventually begin at this beloved castle. Some other fortunate
couple will realize that after everything we mortals
fill our lives with, the only thing that matters is love...*

When the sun rose over Gallant Lake, Amanda's chair
was surrounded with fragile letters scattered across the
floor. She'd dozed a few times during the night, but most
of it had been spent reading. She'd laughed and cried right
along with Madeleine and Otis as they worked at building
the kind of grand love affair that lasted far beyond their own
lives. The letters contained the legacy of Halcyon. They
were a lesson in love and trust. Madeleine was speaking
to her, and she got the message loud and clear. Love was
worth fighting for. Trust isn't always easy, but it's necessary, and it has to be mutual.

She would never betray Blake. How on earth had she
ever thought he could betray her? She'd let her fears and

doubts sabotage her chance at happiness, but she could choose to change that. Loving Blake opened up a future that included laughter and arguments and making up and working together to get through whatever challenges came their way. It was the life she wanted. More than *anything*. And she was willing to fight for it. She *had* to fight for it. She had to fight for them. She and Blake would bring love back to Halcyon.

She pulled her phone from her pocket, desperate to hear Blake's voice. To ask him to forgive her. To tell him she trusted him. The phone sat in her hand for a long time, but she couldn't bring herself to do it. A phone call wasn't enough. She needed to see him. She needed to be looking straight into his dark brown eyes when she told him she was in love with him.

An idea started to warm within her. She couldn't stop smiling while she hustled Zach off to school. As soon as he stepped on the bus, she grabbed her phone again. Her first call went to Julie, then to Jamal.

Amanda plowed ahead before she lost her nerve. "I know you work for Blake, but I need help with something, and Julie said you knew a friend of Blake's who could help us. But I need you *not* to tell Blake about it. Can you do that?"

Jamal was silent for a moment. "In all honesty, Amanda, that depends on what you're talking about."

"I want to surprise him. A *good* surprise. I want to go to this Builders Ball thing, and I need your help to get there without Blake knowing. We had a fight, and I was wrong, and I need to go. I need to see him."

There was silence on the line, and she knew Jamal was struggling between his job duties and his desire to help. Finally he sighed. "It's a very exclusive event, Amanda. You can't just show up at the door. You need to show an invitation, and it's tomorrow night."

Her heart started to fall. Julie said the tickets were in Blake's name.

"Look," Jamal finally said, "my former boss, Andy McCormack, is Mr. Randall's friend. I'm sure Andy's going to the ball. He could get you a ticket. Let me give you his number. If Andy is cool with it, then I'm in."

Chapter Twenty

By noon that same day, the plan was in place. Andy Mc-Cormack was skeptical when she called and introduced herself and her plan. He pointed out that surprises weren't exactly Blake's favorite thing, and this could backfire on all of them. But then he speculated that it might be time for Blake to break free of his No Surprises Lifestyle.

"I've learned life can bring nice surprises in unexpected places," Andy said as a woman giggled in the background. "Blake told me he was going to set up his home base in Gallant Lake. Blake doesn't do home bases. He mentioned this pretty designer who'd turned his world upside down. I'd like him to find the kind of happiness I've found, and I have a hunch you might just be the girl to give it to him. So yes, Amanda, I'll make sure there's a seat for you at our table, which is also Blake's table."

"Oh, Andy, I can't thank you enough. What can you tell me about this party?"

"The event started back at the turn of the last century, when New York City was building up to the sky. The builders, bankers and architects started a foundation to help the less fortunate, and the ball was their major fund-raiser. I'm sure it had a more dignified name originally, but for decades now it's just been the Builders Ball. It's become a massive charity event, raising millions of dollars in just one night. It's very formal. Think black tie times ten. This will be my Caroline's first Builders Ball, too, so you can keep each other company." A woman spoke in the background and Andy laughed. "Caroline says she's wearing a chocolate-colored gown, so you can't wear brown if you're sitting with us… Ow!" More voices in the background. "How the hell was I supposed to know you were kidding? Damn, woman…" More muffled conversation behind a covered phone. Then he was back, and laughing. "Okay, my bride-to-be wants me to tell you we're reserving you a suite at the hotel where the ball is being held so you can get ready there. She can't wait to meet you. She's only talked to Blake once by phone, and she thought he was kind of an asshole. Your willingness to go through all this trouble to surprise him has her reconsidering her assessment. We'll see you there."

She thanked him again and ended the call. Julie had already offered to stay at the house with Zach. It was Friday. The ball was *tomorrow*. She couldn't just show up in an off-the-rack dress and costume jewelry, or she'd embarrass him. She needed a fairy godmother. Or three. She picked up the phone again.

"Mel? I need a fashion miracle, and I need it in twenty-four hours. We'll need Bree's help, too. And Nora. Are you up for a challenge? Good. Here's what's happening…"

Blake looked out over the New York skyline from the penthouse suite of his hotel. The sun was settling low in the afternoon sky. He was going to make his appearance at the gala, shake all the right hands, meet Andy's fiancée, and bolt right after the meal. He was driving home to Halcyon tonight.

He couldn't wait any longer. Amanda was convinced that he'd lied to her about the casino. As angry as he'd been, he understood why her trust was so fragile. Raped at sixteen. Betrayed by a lying, cheating boss. Attacked on the streets of New York. She had a right to be nervous and skeptical. But he wasn't used to having someone doubt him the way she did, and he'd handled it badly.

She didn't trust him because she didn't know how much he loved her. And she didn't know how much he loved her because he hadn't *told* her.

He was in love with the woman, and that's all there was to it. She was the center of his universe. Everything else revolved around that golden-haired woman and his nephew. All that love circling between the three of them and they'd never once discussed it. But tonight he was driving to Halcyon, dropping to his knees and begging her to love him back.

He sipped whiskey from the glass he was holding. If only he knew what the hell she was up to right now. Jamal and Julie had been oddly unavailable since yesterday. Blake called the resort for Jamal three times today to find out if he had any news on some minor vandalism that had been happening around the resort, and Julie kept saying he "just stepped out." Then Jamal would call right back on his cell phone. It was weird. Blake didn't like weird. Blake liked predictable.

He pulled out his phone and called Julie. She'd been his eyes and ears this past week, letting him know that Amanda was okay. She sounded breathless and surprised by his call.

"Blake! Shouldn't you be at your party?"

"I'm heading out shortly." He heard a video game battle going on in the background, and Zach was laughing. "Are you at Halcyon?"

"Oh...yes... I...uh...just stopped by for dinner."

"Is Amanda right there?" The thought of her standing close enough to Julie to take the phone made his heart pound. Maybe he should skip the damned gala and drive home now. Maybe he should talk to her and tell her how he felt.

"Amanda? Oh...uh...no. She's upstairs. She's...um... taking a shower."

"At dinnertime?"

"Yes. She was…working outside this afternoon. She got…um…sweaty."

"What are you having for dinner?"

"Oh, we had pizza at the café…" Before he could question why they had pizza when she'd just said she was at the house for dinner, Julie rushed to correct herself, laughing nervously. "I mean, we had pizza for *lunch*! We were at the café for *lunch*. Not dinner. I think Amanda's making…meat loaf…or something. I'm not really sure, but I know it'll be great."

"Okay." Blake frowned. Things were definitely weird at Gallant Lake. "Is Jamal still down at the office? I was going to give him a call."

"No!" Julie's voice was unusually loud. "I mean…he was going home early tonight. I think he's taking Annie out to dinner for some special occasion or something, so he didn't want to be bothered with calls."

That didn't sound like anything Jamal would ever say. He was always on call. But maybe it was his anniversary or something. Blake rubbed the back of his neck and tried to dismiss his annoyance as he ended the confusing conversation. Julie sounded oddly relieved.

What the hell was going on?

Chapter Twenty-One

Amanda took a deep, shaky breath. What on earth was she doing here in Manhattan? Blake hated surprises, and she was about to show up uninvited. As his date. She shuddered. What if he was with someone else? It was a ridiculous thought, but still. What *would* she do if she walked in and he was there with someone else? She'd die on the spot, that's what she'd do. But she wasn't going to worry about it. She just had to focus on getting ready and finding enough courage to go up to the ballroom.

"Amanda? Are you there?"

Her iPad was propped up on the dresser, and Mel's video call was just coming in. Before Amanda could say anything, another window popped open on the screen. "Amanda? It's Bree, darling. Are you there?"

She jumped in front of the tablet and grinned at her cousins.

"I'm here, girls, and I'm ready for you to make me look fabulous!"

They both applauded, Mel from Miami and Bree from Los Angeles.

Bree responded first. "Oh, sweetie, you already look fabulous! Raquel's been busy, hasn't she?"

Her cousins had pulled out all the stops for her tonight. Mel had called her couture designer friend and a jeweler who owed her a favor. Reality TV star Bree had sent the best hair and makeup artist in the entertainment industry, Raquel Dubois.

Raquel had been hard at work for over an hour, and

Amanda's makeup was flawless. Her hair was piled high on her head. She was wearing a black bustier studded with crystals, and a black lace thong that left little to the imagination. Mel gave her a wolf whistle.

"You look amazing. Go just like that."

They all laughed.

"Girls, I love everything you've done, and I'll owe you forever. But I need your help. I can't decide on a dress, and I'm running out of time. I don't know which one sends the right message."

Bree lifted a glass of wine to her lips. "Well, Mandy, show us the options."

Amanda picked up the tablet and aimed it at the wardrobe rack in her room. "I've narrowed it down to these three. The tight black strapless one, the dark red ball gown with the low, low neckline and no back, or the blue silk with all the draping and the side slit."

"The next question," Mel said, "is what exactly *are* you trying to say? What's your goal here? Make him jealous? Make him sorry? Make him want to jump your bones on the dinner table? What?"

Amanda set the iPad on the dresser and stood in front of it.

"I want to be the woman he loves."

Bree set her wineglass down quickly while Mel coughed.

"Okay, then." It was Bree. "Go with the blue. And, Raquel?"

The beautician stepped into the picture. "Yes, Miss Mathews?"

"Let her hair down. Glue some of those little crystals in it, but just a few. Enough to look dew kissed, but no more. Like you did for Carrie's hair at last month's awards show. And tone down the makeup for a more natural look."

They sorted out her jewelry from the pile of jewelry boxes, settling on a diamond choker, simple drop earrings and a wide gold bracelet studded with tiny diamonds. Mel asked about shoes.

"Black, silver or gold?" Amanda held up one of each.

"The black ones," Bree said. "Bags?"

"I'm carrying that antique bag I bought with Mel in Gallant Lake."

Mel laughed. "That will be perfect!" She had no idea *how* perfect. She had no idea that it was Madeleine Pendleton's cocktail bag. Or that the key they'd all laughed about had unlocked secrets from a century ago.

Amanda felt tears threatening as Raquel unpinned her hair, then pulled some narrow strands back from the side of her face to clip in the back. Large curls fell down over her shoulders. Raquel grabbed a tissue and handed it to her so she could carefully blot under her eyes.

"Don't you dare cry!" Bree called out. "Don't cry until Tall, Dark and Handsome has a chance to see you..."

Another video call rang in. It was Nora, the Atlanta socialite. "Hi, y'all! What did I miss? Oh, my God, Amanda! You look like a movie star! But you still look like *you*. Where's the dress?"

"Hang on and you'll see..." Amanda stepped away from the webcam and into the cobalt blue dress, which hugged her figure in all the right places. When she stepped back in front of the camera, all three cousins squealed together.

"That's it!"

"Oh, my God, you look like a water nymph!"

"Gorgeous!"

She spun in front of them, then caught her reflection in the mirror on the wall. She didn't recognize the elegant woman staring back at her. She'd never worn a fifty-thousand-dollar dress before. And she'd certainly never worn a quarter million in borrowed diamonds. She brushed a strand of hair behind her ear and forced her shoulders back. She could do this. She *had* to do this.

Her phone chirped with a text. It was Caroline Patterson, Andy's fiancée. Just arrived in the ballroom. We're at table four. I'm in dark brown velvet. Blake isn't here yet.

Amanda typed a response. On my way. Wearing blue. She glanced back to the iPad and waved to her cousins.

"This is it, girls. Wish me luck!" She blew them a kiss and pressed the button on the tablet as they all waved and shouted their love to her. Jamal was waiting outside her room, dressed in a tux, and his eyebrows shot to his hairline when he saw her.

"You look stunning, Amanda."

"Thank you, Jamal. Let's hope Blake thinks so."

The ballroom was a glittering wonderland. Table four was on the far side of the dance floor. A laughing brunette was standing there in a skintight brown dress, with auburn hair piled high on her head. Next to her was a tall man with reddish-blond hair and striking blue eyes. The brunette saw Amanda as she was walking across the dance floor and smiled warmly, nudging the good-looking man at her side.

"You must be Amanda! I'm Caroline." She had a soft Southern drawl. "Oh, my God, you look amazing." Caroline gave her a quick squeeze. "This is my fiancé, Andy. He and Blake go way back, and he's been sweating bullets all day about helping you with this little surprise. I hope you know what you're doing."

Amanda shook Andy's hand. "I hope so, too." She barely whispered the words. She was having serious second thoughts. This could go wrong in so many ways. Andy stepped away to speak with two gentlemen who'd called his name. Caroline leaned close, and her accent seemed to thicken.

"If you're trying to knock his socks off, that dress will do it for sure."

Amanda looked at the other woman. "I need him to know how much I love him."

Caroline whistled softly. "You haven't told him how you feel? Well, honey, this is one hell of a place to do it. Andy says the crowd here can be pretty intense. The current and former mayors are here, and the governor is the guest speaker. You've got some balls, girl, if you know what I mean."

A sheen of sweat covered Amanda's skin. If this plan backfired, it would be very public. And it would break her heart. She tried to shake off the clawing panic. "How long have you and Andy been engaged?"

"Only about a month. We're hoping to have the wedding at Blake's Barbados resort next spring. Andy would be happy dashing to Vegas this weekend for a quickie I-do. But I'm my momma's only child, and she wants a real wedding with all the trappings. How can I say no to her?"

Amanda stopped listening somewhere around "dashing to Vegas."

That was the moment Blake walked into the ballroom.

He was alone, which was an enormous relief. He looked tired. Or maybe worried? He shook some man's hand, then turned and looked up. His eyes locked on hers. He froze, and so did she.

"Holy beefcake, Amanda, is that him?" Caroline hissed into her ear.

Amanda could only nod in response.

"No wonder you want him to love you. And look at how he's looking at you... I could melt just from the residual heat over here."

Amanda tried to read all the expressions that ran across Blake's face. Shock. A quick smile. Confusion. Worry. His gaze drifted from her face down the length of her gown and back again. The corner of his mouth slid into a crooked grin. She knew that look. Caroline was right. It was pure molten desire. He started across the floor toward her. A smiling man reached for his hand, but Blake brushed him aside without slowing a beat. His eyes never left hers. Caroline stepped back with a gasp as Blake approached.

Amanda braced herself, forgetting to breathe. Who needed oxygen when she had Blake? He stopped abruptly in front of her, his chest nearly touching her upturned chin. His hands clasped both sides of her face, his face so close that she could feel his breath coming hot and quick. His expression was so intense, so raw, that she almost couldn't bear to look at him. She didn't know how long they stood like that until she heard Andy's voice.

"Make your move, Randall, or walk away. You're turning into the floor show."

People nearby were watching them with surprised curiosity. And still Amanda and Blake stared at each other. His voice was thick with emotion when he finally spoke.

"You tell me you love me, Amanda Lowery." His voice cracked. "Tell me you love me, damn it, because I sure as hell love you."

Relief washed over her.

"I love you." She barely had the words out before his mouth fell on hers, bruising her lips and forcing her teeth apart. His tongue pushed deep, and her hands moved up the front of his tuxedo until her fingers found the lapels and grabbed them.

"Jesus, get a room…" It was Andy again. "Have some dignity, man."

Blake pulled away and Amanda groaned when his lips left hers. They were definitely the center of attention now. She stepped back, her face burning, but he didn't let her go far, keeping his hand tightly on her hip. He held his other hand out to Andy.

"I take it you had something to do with this?"

Andy laughed. "You had me worried right up to that smokin' kiss, my friend. I know you don't like surprises, but Amanda can be very persuasive." Andy pulled Caroline forward. "And this is the girl that made *me* lose all my common sense. Caroline, this is Blake Randall."

Blake released Amanda to put his arms around Caroline. "Great to meet you. He's a lucky guy. Are you still looking at Barbados for the wedding?"

She nodded, looking up at him with a bit of awe. Andy started to grumble.

"Okay, okay, hands off my girl. You've got your own now."

"Yes, I do." He smiled down at her as she moved back to his side. "I do, indeed. Champagne, baby?" He placed a kiss on her forehead. "I'll be right back. You still have some explaining to do."

She grinned as he turned away with a nod to Jamal, who looked relieved. Andy was introducing Caroline to another couple, so she took the opportunity to glance around the ballroom. This was definitely a top-shelf crowd. Her borrowed diamonds had nothing on what some of the women were wearing.

She was supremely grateful for the gown, which was on par with the rest of the expensive dresses in the room. There were plenty of familiar faces from the news and gossip pages among the guests. She spotted Blake standing in line for cocktails near the windows and breathed a sigh of relief. He loved her.

The meal was a blur of rich food and loud laughter. Their table was easily the rowdiest in the ballroom, with Andy and Blake ragging on each other relentlessly. They were like a couple of frat boys, and Amanda loved hearing them tell stories about each other. She and Caroline became fast friends, and the conversation never waned. When the music started, they were the first two couples on the dance floor.

After several songs, Andy offered to switch partners. It was a little odd to feel someone else's hands on her, but she trusted this sun-tanned man with the deep blue eyes.

"Are you okay, Amanda? You seem nervous." His voice was lighter than Blake's, but intense, as if he was ready to leap into battle at any moment.

"I'm fine. I used to have issues about being touched by strangers, but I don't think of you as a stranger. You and Blake are more like brothers than friends, which sort of makes you family."

"I'm an only child, and Blake may as well be, so yes, we are like brothers." He grinned down at her. Blake was dancing nearby with Caroline, but only had eyes for Amanda.

"Thanks for everything you did to make tonight happen."

He gave her a light squeeze, then spun her toward Blake. "You're welcome." He glanced at Blake. "You did good, my friend. She's a keeper."

Blake released Caroline into Andy's arms. "You too, man. We rock."

The two women rolled their eyes in unison as their men laughed.

Jamal was on his phone when they returned to their table, and he didn't look happy. He pulled Blake aside, and Amanda saw Blake's face pale. She went to his side.

"What is it?"

He took her hand, his face grim. "Trouble at the resort. There was a fire at the old clubhouse." The clubhouse was an older building that had been temporarily pulled back into action while the golf course was being expanded and renovated. Blake had shown her the plans for a brand-new structure that would be built on the edge of the lake.

"Was anyone hurt?"

"No, it was after dark when it started." His frown deepened. "They think it was arson."

Amanda stared at him in dismay. The protesters had been a nuisance, but Julie told her things had taken a more aggressive turn recently. Julie had been confronted right on Main Street in town. Jamal said the number of threatening emails and phone calls coming to the resort had jumped sharply. That Russ guy said something about "stopping" Blake. But *arson*? What if they came to the house? She reached for Blake.

"Zach...he and Julie are alone at Halcyon. If someone tries to go to the house..."

Blake pulled her in close and kissed the top of her head.

"We're leaving for Halcyon now. Jamal went to get the car. Zach and Julie are fine. No one's been near the house, and extra security is setting up as we speak."

She followed him out the door without another word.

Amanda was curled up under Blake's arm in the limousine. He pulled her closer and buried his face in her hair. God, he loved the scent of her. He loved the feel of her in his arms. The way she'd laughed as they were dancing.

"You know," he said softly, "right up until the end, that was the best Builders Ball ever. I still can't quite believe you're here."

She chuckled against his chest. "Your reputation for hating surprises had everyone sweating. Andy was afraid it was going to backfire. And poor Jamal was sure he was losing his job."

"And yet you managed to convince them to do it. I definitely need to find a place for you in my company. You're quite the negotiator." He reached down and tipped her chin up so he could see her face. "What made you do all of this? Showing up here... What changed?"

"I learned I was wrong. You were telling the truth about not building the casino. You bought the land to protect Gallant Lake."

He frowned and dropped his hand from her face. He didn't want to renew their argument, but... "But I'd already told you I wasn't building the casino."

She pushed herself upright and stared straight into

his eyes. "I know. And I know it hurt you when I didn't believe you. I'm so sorry about that. More sorry than you can imagine." She dropped her head, and he had to listen closely to hear her next words. "You're nothing like all the men who've betrayed me. I knew that in my heart, but I still..." She looked up, her face crestfallen. "But I still doubted. I was afraid to believe what we had was real. That it could last. That you could possibly feel the same way."

He placed a gentle kiss on her lips, then her nose, then her forehead as she rested her head on his shoulder again. They'd both made so many foolish mistakes. "I'm sorry, too. I lost my temper and stomped away like a spoiled kid. I'd just come off a confrontation with my father and brother, and I took it all out on you. Instead of fighting for us, I walked away. I promise never to do that again."

She lifted her head and stared at him for a long minute. Headlights moved past them outside, flickering across her face. She gave him a crooked grin.

"A friend gave me some really good advice this week."

"Yeah? What advice was that?"

"Well, first she made me understand that I shouldn't expect your feelings to be any less than mine. If I would never betray *you*, then it was cruel to think that you could betray *me*. Then she told me that 'after everything we mortals fill our lives with, the only thing that matters is love.' After hearing that, I realized I had to make sure you knew how much I loved you."

He took a deep breath to slow his pounding heart. "Smart friend. Who was she?"

"Hmm? Oh, I don't think you've met her..."

With a quick move, he scooped her up and set her across his lap. He needed her in his arms. Forever.

"Careful!" she yelped as she adjusted her dress. "All of this stuff is borrowed, so don't tear the dress. I turn into a pumpkin at midnight."

He ran his hands down the bodice of the dark blue gown. "I like this dress. I think we'll buy it." He held up her hand so the bracelet twinkled in the reflection of the headlights of cars around them. "I like this, too. Let's keep it. The rest we can take care of tomorrow. And don't worry, I won't let anyone turn you into a pumpkin or anything else, Mandy."

"Mandy? I don't think you've called me that before." She tipped her head to the side and grinned at him.

"Isn't that what your family calls you?"

"Sometimes. It's a nickname Nora started. I like how it sounds on your lips."

"Okay, then. *Mandy*, snuggle into me and get some rest. We've got another hour or so before we're home."

She obliged with a sigh. "Our home. It's a dream come true, Blake."

"*You're* the dream come true, sweetheart." He kissed the top of her head and waited until her steady breathing told him she was asleep. Then he lowered the window dividing the back of the limousine from the front. Jamal was behind the wheel.

"Any news?" Blake asked quietly.

Jamal shook his head. "Deputy Sheriff Adams is running the official investigation. No one suspicious has been near the house or the resort. Tim and Bobby are both camping out on sofas at Halcyon tonight while Julie and Zach are asleep. Plus we have the usual staff outside. There are a couple construction guys coming in on Monday to wrap things up, and then they're done, so we won't have to worry about that traffic in and out."

Blake pressed a thoughtful kiss on the top of Amanda's sleeping head. He needed to put out a statement this week about canceling the casino plans. He'd only held off because he wanted to have an alternative to present to appease both his investors and the people hoping for jobs.

He glanced down at Amanda again. This wasn't about

business and investors anymore. This was about protecting the people he loved. The situation seemed to be under as much control as possible at this point.

So why did he still feel so uneasy?

Chapter Twenty-Two

Amanda welcomed Sunday morning with a cup of coffee on the balcony outside the master suite at Halcyon. Someone was walking through the trees. She held her breath until she recognized Tim from the security team. There were people guarding Halcyon night and day now, keeping any possible troublemakers away. The Gallant Lake Preservation Society was cooperating with the investigation, insisting they had nothing to do with the recent acts of vandalism and arson.

"Hey, you." Blake's deep voice made her skin heat up. She turned to the doorway and grinned.

"Hey, yourself. Good morning." He draped his arm over her shoulders and kissed her temple. She tipped her face up and he dropped a chaste kiss on her lips. They were relaxed with each other at last. Comfortable. No longer trying to prove anything. It was a revelation to her that she could be this thoroughly content.

He nibbled her bottom lip and grumbled. "You're daydreaming while I'm kissing you. Am I boring you?"

"I'm daydreaming about how much I love you." She felt him smile against her mouth.

"Well, in that case, I'll allow it."

He raised his head and noticed the coffee she was still clutching.

"And you didn't spill a drop. I'm impressed with your focus, Miss Lowery." His sable eyes met hers. "What are you planning to tackle today?"

"I want to draw up plans for the guest rooms on the second floor. Are you up for some real construction? I'm thinking of knocking down a few walls to make larger rooms. It's not like we really need twelve bedrooms, and those rooms are so small."

He nodded. "Make all the plans you want, but wait until after the holidays to tear things apart, okay?"

"Which holiday? Thanksgiving is only a couple weeks away."

Blake gave her a squeeze. "I don't think even you could get a renovation done by Thanksgiving. I was referring to Christmas."

"Why? Does Santa have big plans?" Christmas had never been a very happy time for her since her dad died. And Zach—his mom died last Christmas. Maybe it *was* time to make new memories.

He laughed. "Yeah, something like that." He looked like he was keeping a secret. What was he up to? And what on earth would she ever give him for Christmas?

She kissed his cheek playfully. "Don't forget that Zach has a birthday party to go to this afternoon. He's really excited about it."

"How could I possibly forget? It's all he's talked about. A party at the arcade in the next town, complete with laser tag. It's every ten-year-old's dream."

She saw just a brief shadow cross his face, and she knew he was thinking about all the rowdy birthday parties he never had as a child. She rested her palm against his cheek. "Zach's birthday is next spring, and we'll make sure he has the wildest birthday party ever seen in Gallant Lake. And Uncle Blake will be able to ride the ponies and play laser tag and dress up like a pirate and be just like all the other little kids."

He laughed out loud and pulled her tightly into his arms. "I'm going to hold you to that, Miss Amanda."

She knew they were in for a long night as soon as Zach got home from the party. He'd clearly had way too much ice cream, along with who knows what other junk food. He'd been laughing when he'd arrived home, but she could almost see the greenish tinge to his skin. He rubbed his stomach absently while he watched television with her and Blake.

It was no surprise when she heard her name being called in the middle of the night. Blake barely registered her exit from their bed, rolling over with a grunt. She pulled her bathrobe tight and trotted down the hall, finding Zach on his knees in his bathroom. It wasn't a pretty sight. *Welcome to parenthood, Amanda.* She soaked a washcloth in cold water and held it against his forehead as he threw up. She rubbed his back and cooed words of comfort to him for two hours, until he finally seemed to have purged all the garbage from his system. He begged her not to leave, so she curled up with him in his bed where they both drifted into an exhausted sleep.

That's where Blake found them Monday morning. She woke when he pressed his lips to her temple. Zach was still sound asleep. She looked from the clock to Zach's pale face and knew there was no way he was making it to school today. She put her finger to her lips to silence Blake and slid out of bed gently. Once they were out in the hall, he spoke.

"I woke up and you were gone. What happened?"

"All that junk food caught up with him in the middle of the night. I didn't want to wake you. I know you have that conference today." Blake had scheduled a video conference with the resort managers to discuss how best to restructure the chain of command so that he could operate the company with fewer personal visits to the resorts. He was releasing some of his tight control, and she knew that wasn't easy for him. He grinned down at her and brushed her hair behind her ear.

"Thanks, babe. I promise I'll make it up to you. Are they finishing up in the office today?"

"Yes. They just need to put up the last of the crown molding. One last chance for me to climb a ladder..."

He arched a brow at her, and she thought for the thousandth time how lucky she was to fall in love with such a gorgeous man. He was dressed for business today, in a dark suit and gleaming white dress shirt. His black hair curled over the collar, and she couldn't resist putting her fingers in it.

She pulled his head lower. "I'm just teasing you. Go have your meeting. I'll see you later." The kiss was lingering and sweet.

"Take good care of our patient." He winked at her before turning away. Bobby and his crew were hammering away downstairs, so she headed to the suite to shower and dress before she went down to the main floor.

Zach was awake by the time she'd dressed, and she ordered him to stay in his room, promising to deliver a light breakfast.

"It's hard to believe it's the same house, Bobby." She stood in the main hall a few hours later and looked around. Her sketches had come to life, and so had Halcyon.

"You were the brains of the operation, Amanda. I just supplied the muscle." Bobby grinned at her. "I know you want to start the second-floor demolition, but Blake said it will have to wait until after the holidays." She shook her head. She knew he wanted to give Zach a wonderful Christmas, and figured he was planning something big.

She and Bobby hugged and she waved goodbye to the workers as they filed out. She fixed a cup of soup for Zach's lunch and was just heading toward the stairs with it when she heard the front door open. She turned, expecting to see Blake, or maybe Bobby. But it was Russ, the one who'd said Blake needed to be stopped. Her stomach dropped.

She started to ask what he was doing there, but her words froze in her throat when he turned to lock the front door.

He'd probably walked right past security, since he'd been working on the house. He was only a few feet away, and when he turned back to face her, the malice and madness were clear in his eyes. In his left hand was a red container of gasoline. In his right hand was a gun, and it was aimed straight at her.

RUN!

The warning voice screamed in her head, but she couldn't move. It wasn't a panic attack that rendered her motionless. It was the thought of Zach upstairs. She blinked and tried to focus, setting the soup on an end table with trembling hands.

"I… I don't understand." She moved away from the stairs toward the center of the room. She didn't want him leaving the main floor. "What do you want, Russ? What are you doing?"

"I want your boyfriend to leave my town alone. To leave my family alone." He moved closer. She started to step back and he raised the gun. She froze. The scent of stale cigarette smoke assaulted her senses, and she placed a hand over her roiling stomach. His gray eyes were narrow and cold.

"Y-your family?" Amanda stuttered.

"Randall bought out my parents' farm. And my uncle's place, too. Been in the family for decades. Those places should have come to my cousins and me, not some New York City developer. What the hell does he want with it all? Those are worthless pieces of land to anyone other than us."

Blake had been buying land all around Gallant Lake to keep his family from developing it. But he was only buying what was already for sale.

"Didn't your family have the farms for sale?"

The man scoffed. "Sure, there were for-sale signs up, but no one was gonna buy them. No one wanted to buy *anything* in Gallant Lake until Randall showed up and started all his big casino talk. Eventually my parents would have died and it would come to us. Now we have *nothing*. And it's not just us. Other guys have had their inheritances robbed from them, too. We decided to fight back."

"But…your families *wanted* to sell, and got fair market value…"

"We needed that land! It was *ours*! And Randall *took* it from us! Now I'm gonna take something from him." He looked around the hall.

Think, Amanda! This is no time for panic…

"Look, Blake's not building the casino anymore," she managed to say as her mind raced. "He changed his mind…"

"Yeah, I heard that rumor, too, but I don't believe it. And he still owns the land I need to make a living."

"You made your living off the farm? Then why did your parents—"

"They didn't *know* what we were growing back on the hill. They didn't know what we were cooking in the barn on Harrison's old place. And now it's all gone, thanks to your big man from the city. And it's time for some payback."

This wasn't about the casino. Blake probably had no idea he'd stepped in the middle of some small-town drug ring in his attempt to save Gallant Lake.

She concentrated on keeping her breathing slow and steady. A sheen of sweat blossomed across her skin. Russ stepped closer, but she forced herself to stand her ground and look him in the eye. She was tired of being afraid. She was done with it. If she was going to die here, she was going to do it without showing fear.

"You'll go to prison for this."

He looked around the room. "Nah. By the time they see the old place going up in flames, I'll be long gone."

He was going to set fire to Halcyon. With her and Zach inside. She had to think of some way out of this. She had to stop him.

"That's a terrible idea. Even if Blake leaves, he still owns your land. You still lose."

"I figure he'll be more than happy to dump that land, just to get out of town and be done with it. And we've got partners ready to snap it up." Russ gestured toward the stairs with the handgun.

"Come on. We'll start upstairs, where they'll find your body. Then I'll burn my way down and walk away."

"Miss Amanda? I'm hungry..."

Zach stood at the turn of the staircase. He looked from her to Russ in confusion. His eyes went wide when he saw the gun. Russ stared up at Zach. He moved to point the gun toward the boy with a thin, frightening smirk.

"Amanda?" Zach's voice was high and thin. A surge of adrenaline coursed through Amanda's body as she shouted. At the same time, she leaped toward Russ.

"Zach! *Run!*"

Russ's attention snapped back to her and he struck her on the side of her head with the butt of the gun. Everything went black for a moment. She staggered but stayed on her feet.

"Run, Zach!"

His footsteps pounded up the stairs. There was a back staircase he could use to escape, or even the small elevator. He had options from upstairs if she just gave him some time. She clawed at Russ and he hit her again. She fell to her knees, but got back up, fueled by anger and desperation. She put herself between him and the staircase. He gave her a look of contempt and roughly pushed her aside as he headed to the stairs.

"What a tragedy that a woman and boy died together in the fire."

Blake would never survive losing them both.

She had to fight. She grabbed at Russ and held on to his shirt, slowing his progress as he put his foot on the stairs. They wrestled like that all the way to the third floor. When she and Russ both tumbled into the hallway on the third floor, she started to beg.

"Please! He's just a boy!"

"Yeah. *Randall's* boy." He held the gun up to the side of her head and she held her breath. "I'll find him easier without you swattin' at me the whole time."

The silence was heavy and tense, broken only by her ragged breathing. The cold barrel of the gun pressed against her temple. This was it. She imagined she could hear the trigger starting to move, and she offered a silent prayer that Zach would get to Blake somehow and be safe.

A door shut loudly inside Zach's room, making them both flinch. Russ's head snapped around, and he shoved her to the floor. "I'm going to finish that brat before he gets out of here."

He ran down the hall and kicked open the door to Zach's room, ignoring Amanda's screams for him to stop. She was hot on his heels. The bedroom was empty. The bathroom door was open but it was empty, too. She watched, gasping for breath, as Russ stood in the center of the room, spinning wildly to point the barrel of his gun from door to door. He stopped when he faced the closet.

With a sinking heart, Amanda realized the same thing Russ did. The closet was the only place to hide in this room. Zach had to be in there. She leaped toward the closet door as Russ raised the gun and pulled the trigger. Again. And again.

The roar was deafening, and the shock of the sound seemed to suspend time somehow. Amanda was vividly aware of her body flying horizontally in front of the closet door. She felt the first bullet slice into her left arm. The pain was sharp and clean, like a razor's cut. But the pain of the next strike was different. The bullet struck her abdomen, just right of center, and the burning was so intense she knew she had to be dying. She could hear her own screams as if they were coming from somewhere far away. All she could see was red when she hit the floor. She felt the warmth and wetness of her own blood on her fingers. She couldn't move, paralyzed with shock and pain.

Russ stepped over her to open the closet door. She turned her head. She wanted Zach to know he wasn't going to die alone.

But the closet was empty. Her eyes closed in relief. She was the one who would die alone. That was okay. As long as Zachary lived. Relief washed over her. Another door slammed somewhere inside the house. Was it Zach? Russ was already running into the hall.

She gritted her teeth and forced herself to her feet, with her right hand clutching her bleeding abdomen. She made it around the corner of the hallway before her legs betrayed her and she collapsed against the wall, sliding to the floor. She screamed Zach's name one last time, but the sound barely escaped her dry lips. She watched the action as if through the wrong end of a telescope, out of focus and far, far away. Russ was running for the stairs.

And then he was just…gone.

Men were shouting somewhere. Blake called her name, but she couldn't answer. Her world was growing darker, and so much colder. Jamal was saying they "had him." More pounding steps, then Blake was holding her.

"Amanda!" His voice shook, then he shouted loudly. "She's been shot! Get an ambulance!" His trembling lips settled softly on her forehead and he began to plead as he rocked her in his arms. "Don't leave me, baby. Help is coming. Please stay with me…"

"Zach?" It took the last of her strength to whisper the name.

"He's safe. He came to get me. Amanda… Amanda? Oh, God…no…" His voice cracked as everything she knew faded to blackness and silence.

Chapter Twenty-Three

Blake had always adored Amanda's petite build, but not now. Not when it made her look so tiny and fragile in the hospital bed. She was ghostly pale, with tubes and wires everywhere around her. Her long hair was pulled to one side and cascaded over her shoulder in a golden ponytail, having been lovingly brushed and secured by Nora.

Her cousins had arrived yesterday, and were holding their vigil in the waiting room, taking turns sitting with Blake. But once in a while they gave him time alone with her. Time to grieve and pray and plead with whomever was in charge upstairs to give him more time with the woman he loved. He made promises. Vowed to change. Vowed to make peace with his family if that's what it took to bring her back. Give up his businesses. Become a missionary in Africa.

He'd do anything.

Anything.

ANYTHING.

He rested his forehead on the back of her hand, which he was clutching tightly in his own. A large hand settled on his shoulder. He looked up to find Andy standing at his side. Caroline was behind him, tears brimming in her eyes. Could it be that just a few days ago they were all laughing together at the Builders Ball? Andy stared at Amanda, clenching his jaw so tightly that a muscle in his cheek twitched. It was Caroline who spoke first.

"She's strong, Blake. So strong. I could see it the minute I met her."

Andy gave his shoulder a squeeze.

"Thanks, guys." His voice sounded foreign to his own ears, raspy from exhaustion and tears.

"Julie's got the resort under control," Andy said quietly. "The business is fine." The video conference had ended abruptly when Zach ran screaming into the conference room. That was two days ago. Two days that felt like a lifetime.

"What do you need, Blake?" Caroline's voice was soft.

That was easy to answer. There was only one thing.

"I need her to wake up. She lost so much blood..." He reached up and touched his fingers to Amanda's still face.

"Give her body time to heal," Andy said. "She'll come back. Don't give up." He sat in a nearby chair and pulled Caroline down onto his knee. "The bastard who did this is in jail?"

"Right now he's in the hospital, but he's headed to jail after that."

"Why is he in the hospital?"

"He fell down the stairs. Cracked his skull and broke his leg." Blake looked at Amanda. "He keeps insisting someone pushed him, but Amanda was nowhere near the stairs when I got there."

Blake lifted her hand and kissed it. None of it mattered right now. He just wanted her to wake up for him. He wanted her back.

Andy continued softly. "Dan Adams told me they found a meth lab Russ and his cousins were running. It was quite an operation. He'll be in jail a long time, Blake."

"I don't give a damn about him right now. I just want her back. I want her back..."

He dropped his head to her hand again and sighed. He was vaguely aware that Andy and Caroline were still sitting there, silent sentinels and loyal friends. He was so dog-tired his whole body ached from it. It wasn't just lack of sleep. It was anger and grief and worry that were draining him.

He wanted his girl back.

Amanda's thoughts were dark and murky. Fragments of awareness fought to come together, but they couldn't quite get there. She wanted to open her eyes, but they wouldn't cooperate. She wanted to beg for something to drink, but her dry lips were just as uncooperative and would not move. Once in a while she heard sounds, but nothing that made sense. Words came through in bits and pieces, and if more than one person spoke, the voices blended together into an annoying, foreign-sounding mess. She heard Blake's voice once, and it sounded like he was…what? Begging? Praying? She thought she felt tears on her hand, but she couldn't move it, couldn't open her eyes, didn't know whose tears they were. She had no sense of time, and didn't know if she'd been trapped in this darkness for hours or days. There was a distant, pounding ache in her side that presented a constant backbeat to her thoughts. Sometimes she wanted to cry from the pain, but even her tears refused to follow orders.

And then, as if on command from some other power, her eyes swept open. She blinked quickly and tried to assess where she was. A machine was beeping quietly next to her. The room was dark, with only one soft light over the bed. She slowly turned her head. She was in a hospital room. The pain in her side was no longer in the background. It was sharp and insistent.

Everything came back to her in a rush. She'd been shot. She took a deep breath and reveled in the feeling of air moving in and out of her lungs. She was alive. She was *alive*.

"Blake, she's awake…" A woman's whispered words caught her attention. There was a sudden movement at her side, and Blake's beautiful, wonderful, handsome face appeared directly over hers. He looked so tired. His eyes were tense, and there were deep, dark bags under them. His hair was a mess, and his skin was pale. But love shone from him like a warm blanket, and she grinned up at him.

"Wow." Her voice cracked. "Do I look as bad as you do?"

He took a sharp breath, clearly unprepared for humor. Then he slowly returned her smile.

"You look perfect, baby." He dropped a kiss on her forehead and stayed there for a moment, trembling lips pressed to her skin, as if he was trying to compose himself. "You look absolutely perfect. You came back to me."

"Zach's okay?"

He smiled against her skin. "Zach's fine."

His lips brushed against hers reverently, their noses touching. Caroline and Andy stood, and Caroline winked at Amanda. "We'll give you some time alone, and let the others know you're awake."

And they were gone. Blake gave her a much-needed sip of water, then sat back in his chair and held her hand. He ran kisses across her palm and down to her wrist, pressing his lips on her pulse point.

"For two days, I've been kissing this spot over and over, just to feel your heartbeat. I thought I'd lost you..." His voice cracked, and she lifted her fingers to touch his face.

"Tell me what happened. How did Zach escape? What happened to...that man?"

"You should rest..."

"I need to know." Her voice was stronger now. She had to put the pieces together in her head.

He sat back and looked over his shoulder. "Andy will try to give us privacy, but your cousins will only wait so long..."

Her cousins were here? She narrowed her eyes. He was trying to distract her.

"Then you'd better start talking. I need to put my memories in order, Blake. There are too many holes, and nothing makes sense."

"Okay, okay." He started talking quickly, as if the memories were no fun for him. "Zach ran to his room after he saw you downstairs. When he ran into the bedroom, he saw a small panel open next to the fireplace that he'd never noticed before. Talk about perfect timing. It was a secret passageway that had been built into the house, with a hidden stairway.

"He started down the stairs, then he heard you and Garrity fighting." He noticed her look of confusion and explained, "Russ Garrity. The son of a bitch who tried to kill you."

She remembered now. "It was all about drugs, Blake. Not the casino. Drugs…"

"I know, babe. The sheriff knows, too. Russ and his cousins are looking at serious time."

"What happened with Zach?"

"He turned back. He was going to try to save you." Amanda closed her eyes in horror at the thought. "He insists that's when he heard his mother's voice, as if she were standing right next to him, telling him to find me fast. He ran down to the resort, screaming bloody murder about a man with a gun." Blake's face paled even more.

"I barely remember racing up to Halcyon. Jamal and I unlocked the front door as gunfire rang out. A piece of me died right then. We came in to the sound of more shots, and I heard you screaming. It was a beautiful sound, because at least I knew you were alive. We ran up the stairs, and found Garrity halfway down the staircase. Jamal grabbed the gun while I ran up and found you in the hall…" His voice trailed off. She could only imagine what he saw. He took a breath and continued. "There was so much blood. The blood loss is what nearly killed you." He clutched her hand and brushed his lips across his knuckles. "The bullet grazed your liver. But it also nicked an artery, and when you forced yourself to move, the bleeding…"

"We heard a door slam. Maybe it was you and Jamal coming in." She smiled. "Or maybe it was a ghost."

"Yeah, right. Would have been nice if our so-called ghost showed up *before* you got shot."

"I thought it was Zach. I tried to save him, but I collapsed before I could do anything." Amanda's eyes closed for a moment, overwhelmed at the thought of how close they came to disaster.

"Amanda, please don't close your eyes. Look at me. I've waited two days to see those beautiful blue eyes of yours."

She blinked away the tears that threatened to fall. She knew he hadn't left her side. She reached out to him with her left hand and winced at the jolt of pain she felt.

"That's just a flesh wound on your arm. It'll heal in no time."

But something else caught her attention and she didn't register what he was saying. There was a ring sparkling on her left hand. It was a glittering canary diamond in a pillow setting, surrounded with small white diamonds, all supported in a lacy platinum setting that fit her small hand perfectly. Blake lifted a shoulder when she met his loving eyes.

"It's a golden diamond for my golden girl. I was going to propose this weekend at Halcyon. I figured we could have a Christmas wedding. When I wasn't sure…" His face darkened, and he looked as if he were in physical pain. He swallowed hard. "I wanted you to be wearing it, you know? In case something happened." He took a deep breath and said the next part quickly. "If you died, I wanted to be sure you were mine. I wanted you to be my fiancée before you left me…" Her heart pounded so loudly she thought he'd hear it. She couldn't imagine what he'd gone through while she was unconscious. He seemed lost in somber thought, then he looked up and gave her a boyish grin.

"I think I knew we'd be together from that first day when I caught you breaking into my house. You were so beautiful and so full of…life. When I watched you sleeping in my bed that day, I thought I'd stepped into a fairy tale."

She laughed, and grimaced at the pain it caused. "I didn't break in. The door was wide-open."

"Whatever." He chuckled. "Even when you drove me crazy and challenged me and flat out defied me…even then, I just couldn't stay away from you. I know this sounds sappy, but I was the moth to your flame." She rolled her eyes, but he kept going. "I'm *serious*. You didn't hesitate to call me out when I was being an idiot, or when I was being a coward, or when I was in denial. I told you I didn't believe in love, and you made me see what a lie that was. You rebuilt me, Amanda, from the ground up. I thought I hated surprises, but you've surprised me at every turn. I want to spend the rest of my life looking forward to the next surprise you have in store, whether it's orange chandeliers…"

"Paprika," she protested softly. She felt a tear escape the corner of her eye and roll down her cheek.

"…or little boys on my doorstep that you won't let me discard. You told me once that I saw you whole. Well, you *made* me whole, my love. The ghosts from our pasts can't hurt us anymore." He got up from the chair and gave her a soft kiss. "And the ghosts from Halcyon's past are on our side. Marry me, Amanda. Marry me."

A rising hum of voices was building outside the door to her room. He dropped to one knee at the side of her bed, still holding her hand.

"Say 'yes' before we're invaded by all the other people who love you."

"Blake, from the first moment you touched me, you've made me feel safe. I know I fought you and panicked and occasionally tried to chase you away—" he smiled at that "—but you kept insisting what we had was right and true. And it was. It *is*. I'm done with being afraid. Life is waiting for us both, Blake, and I can't imagine facing it without you. I love you, and—"

His mouth was on hers before she could finish. Insistent, tender, passionate and protective. Everything that *he* was, that's what his kiss was. There was love there. There was security there. And as she parted her lips with a sigh of surrender, she knew without a doubt there would be arguments and laughter and passion and challenges and common enemies and many, many friends in their future. There would be babies for sure, and there would be Halcyon. But most important was the love they shared. Her right hand rose and twisted in his curling black hair. He growled as she tugged him closer. He was hers. She was his. No more secrets. No more fear. Only love.

They were barely aware of the door to the room pushing open. Nora stepped in, then raised her hand to silence the group behind her. Julie held Zach's shoulders tightly to keep him from dashing forward. With her were Mel, Bree, Andy, Caroline and, yes, even Dario, weeping loudly into his handkerchief. They stopped en masse and waited for the kiss to finally end before flooding into the room to welcome Amanda back to the world of the living.

Epilogue

Blake fidgeted with the collar of his gray morning suit. Damn Amanda for insisting on the formality. And damn him for not being able to say no to her. Zachary shifted at his side, and dug his fingers under the collar of his own matching suit. Blake winked at him, but Zach just rolled his eyes.

"How much longer, Dad?"

He was Blake's best man, clutching two wedding rings tightly in his hand. Blake and Amanda began the adoption process last month, with Zach's blessing. He'd never had a father, and he got such a kick out of calling Blake "Dad." That was nothing compared to what Blake felt every time he heard it. The boy needed security and stability, and he'd have that as their son. Amanda had no intention of replacing Tiffany, and she'd insisted he call her "Aunt Amanda." But Zach argued that once she married his *dad*, then she'd be his mom. His second mom.

Andy hovered nearby, laughing with Caroline about something. He was probably gloating over the fact *he* didn't have to wear a silly tux. A small crowd was gathered in Halcyon's main hall, which had been transformed into a Christmas wonderland. The tree stretched to the high ceiling at one end of the room, covered with hundreds of twinkling lights. The ornaments were all colors and shapes. Amanda wanted a giant, old-fashioned tree, and she got it. Their gifts had all been opened on Christmas morning, then whisked out of sight in preparation for the wedding.

Pine boughs were wrapped through the chandeliers and draped across every surface downstairs. Amanda chose an ivory and pink color theme for the wedding, and Halcyon was glowing like a candy confection. The marble fireplace had been transformed into an altar, complete with a large brass cross Amanda found in the attic. Ivory and pink roses fell in a beribboned blanket from the mantel to the floor. A string quartet was set up in front of the tree, playing a soft medley of Christmas music and love songs.

Blake caught a movement on the stairs and turned as Amanda's cousins came down the steps in one giggling mass of pink silk and ivory velvet. Amanda wanted to keep things small and refused to choose only one cousin to be an attendant, so the three of them were dubbed "the women in charge." Bree coordinated the decor and logistics, Mel helped create the gown, and Nora worked with Dario on the menu. The three women had been upstairs helping the bride with last-minute preparations.

Bree nodded to the quartet, and they stopped playing. People moved to take their seats near the makeshift altar. A man in a black tuxedo sat at the new grand piano that had been Blake's Christmas gift to Amanda. With a gesture from Bree, the guests stood and turned to face the staircase. The pianist paused, then played the Vangelis hymn Amanda had chosen. Blake rested his hand on Zach's shoulder. The moment had arrived, and not a moment too soon. No one else in this room had any idea how fortuitous their short engagement had proven to be.

Julie stepped into view on the stairs. Her hair was pinned demurely behind each ear with jeweled clips. The pale pink gown showed off her freckled skin. She beamed at Zach before turning her smile to Blake as she moved to stand across from them.

The entire room sighed when Amanda rounded the corner of the staircase. Her hair was piled high on her head, with a few tendrils curling down her back. She held a small spray of pink and ivory roses. When they'd found Madeleine's old wedding gown in the attic, Amanda immediately sent it to Mel to be used as part of her own gown, and Mel's designer friend had worked wonders. The century-old hand-beaded Irish lace was draped and gathered over a cream satin sheath that hugged Amanda's curves perfectly. She looked like a vision from a very grown-up fairy tale as she walked toward Blake. The neckline draped low, highlighting breasts that threatened to overflow the satin bodice. Was it possible they were already getting bigger?

There was amusement in her eyes when he looked back to her face. She knew he'd been checking her out, and she certainly knew why. They grinned at each other like a couple of lovestruck teenagers, shy and adoring. She rested her hand in his and they turned to the pastor. Blake had a hard time focusing on the words being said, because he couldn't take his eyes off his beautiful bride.

He was in love. Forever love. The kind of love that songs were written about. The kind of love he'd never believed in until Amanda Lowery walked into his house and his life. He was one lucky bastard.

Amanda went to their suite to freshen up after the wedding meal. She was tired, and she'd had a rough morning before she started to get ready for the ceremony. But she was also blissfully happy. She headed back down the stairs. *Blissful.* There was a word she rarely thought of, much less used. But it was perfect for what she was feeling today. Sure, she still felt a little green around the gills, and throwing up every morning was no fun with her wound still healing. But the doctor had assured them there was nothing to worry about.

She was Mrs. Blake Randall. It was hard to remember what her life had been like before she met him. They were new people now, and they were building a new family here in Halcyon. She rounded the final turn of the staircase and stopped to gaze fondly at the people gathered for the wedding celebration. A DJ was playing music, and people were dancing in the living room, which had been cleared of most of its furniture for the occasion. The cake had been cut, the flowers had been tossed, the garter had been thrown. Now she could relax and enjoy the festivities.

Blake stood talking to Julie and Bobby near the Christmas tree. This was an intimate gathering of friends and associates. Other than Amanda's cousins, there were no family members here. Her mom was terrified of flying, and they'd promised to visit her in Kansas soon. Blake's family wasn't even an option. Despite that, or maybe because of it, the hall was bursting with love.

Her husband smiled across the hall at her when she caught his eye. Unconsciously, her hand traveled to her stomach, and he followed the movement. He looked back to her face, his smile deepening. He knew exactly what was growing there—his Christmas present. They hadn't told anyone—it was too soon, and it was a bit awkward with the wedding and all. But at nine weeks, her morning sickness was beginning to fade and her body was adjusting to the new life beginning deep in her womb. Her doctor was confident the pregnancy would proceed without complication.

It had been a shock to receive the news in the hospital that she was expecting. Amanda kept insisting it was impossible, but the doctor pointed out that even the best birth control methods failed sometimes. Madeleine Tiffany Randall had survived the shooting and seemed to be thriving.

Blake teased Amanda about the name choice, asking if she intended to name the baby Otis if it was a boy. But she knew this was a girl. It was *their* little girl. Zach's new sister.

Their little Maddy. She walked down a few more steps and glanced toward the fireplace, where several clusters of guests were talking. As one group moved away, she noticed two women standing together near the rose-covered mantel. They made a curious pair.

The older woman had golden hair, pulled into a bun that rested low on her neck. She was wearing an elegant blue satin gown that looked straight out of a silent Hollywood movie from the 1920s. The younger woman had long ebony hair, braided and intertwined with colorful ribbons. Her flowing dress was gathered under her breasts with another ribbon. She looked bohemian, free-spirited and very contemporary. The two women turned together to face her, and Amanda stopped breathing, bringing her hand to her throat. The young woman had Blake's dark sable eyes, flecked with gold. She smiled, and Amanda recognized Zach in her open, trusting grin. The older woman dipped her head in her direction. Amanda had seen her before, of course, in the picture that hung in the upstairs hallway. It was a photograph of Madeleine Pendleton that was dated 1925.

"Amanda? Are you okay?" Blake was suddenly at her side on the stairs. "You look a little pale. Is our daughter dancing the tarantella again?" She looked up into his laughing eyes. He insisted her morning sickness was due to his healthy offspring dancing in her tummy, even though the baby was barely bigger than a kidney bean at this point.

"I just saw…" She glanced to the fireplace. The women were gone. Maybe she'd imagined it. Or maybe Madeleine and Tiffany showed up to give their blessing to this happy family.

"You saw what, baby?"

She went on tiptoe to place a kiss on Blake's lips. "I saw the future, sweetheart," she said to her husband. "And it's going to be wonderful."

"I don't doubt it. Not for one minute." He took her hand and walked her down the remaining stairs.

"Come dance with me, Mrs. Randall."

"Forever, Mr. Randall."

And she did.

* * * * *